CW01638989

Jacqueline Cottrell

VIXSTORY

With all best wishes
to one of my greatest
fans!

Limited Special Edition. No. 5 of 25 Paperbacks

As ever,
Jacq.

Jacqueline was born in London and studied at UEA in Norwich and Goldsmiths in London. After a career in education, she developed businesses in the West Country of England and enjoyed a portfolio of community engagement and literary activities. Jacqueline is married with one son and now lives in Hampshire. This is her first novel, with a second due out later in the year.

For Alan and Nick, with love.

In memory of James Norman Daynes, a great storyteller, who died on the 21st of October 2010; and of course, for Iris, who left us her imagination.

Jacqueline Cottrell

VIXSTORY

AUSTIN MACAULEY PUBLISHERS™
LONDON • CAMBRIDGE • NEW YORK • SHARJAH

A CIP catalogue record for this title is available from the British Library.

ISBN 9781528972482 (Paperback)
ISBN 9781528973953 (ePub e-book)

www.austinmacauley.com

First Published (2019)
Austin Macauley Publishers Ltd
25 Canada Square
Canary Wharf
London
E14 5LQ

The Portsmouth History Centre – a great local resource. My Somerset writing buddies for encouragement and, of course, my wonderful editor, Alan Cottrell.

Prologue

Dr Stanley strode in. He was wearing his Harris Tweed jacket and his little eyes danced around the assembled gathering, his coterie of young things, female things, so eager to learn, so very interested in his little experiments into the afterlife. His regression experiences certainly attracted them and he enjoyed the attention, the proximity and the opportunity it all presented to him. It was nice to step out of the shadows for once in his career,

The young woman volunteer lay perfectly still, breathing quietly despite the apprehension in her eyes. She was pale, understandably, and communicated very little. She appeared accepting of the unusual situation in which she found herself and so, was probably ideal for his purposes. He smiled down at her and then across to the small gathering of researchers, his eyes glinting, his lips relying to speak.

Two colleagues stood by, witnessing the scene as they had done before with others, although the woman volunteer today was well known to one of them.

"Do you ever get the feeling you might have made a mistake?" She kept her eyes on her friend as she spoke in conspiratorial whispers.

"Never darling," he stared hard at her but without malice in his look.

"You don't need to camp it up with me you know, darling."

"I like it. Leave me alone. It's my persona, in plain sight as they say."

"It will get you noticed."

"I rest my case," as he said, his smile was boyish. "It might, I won't. Anyway, I'm off, Calypso calls."

"Let us begin," Dr Stanley announced as the lights dimmed, "Vix story."

Chapter 1
Portsmouth, 1805

I could hear them before I could see them. First the musical sounds of fiddle and voice, then the loud raucous laughter, some shrill, some deep and some altogether strange and heathen; unfamiliar even to me.

But it was a good day. I turned out of the alleyway before the dock, walking into the soft sunlight of the late afternoon as it escaped through the great tall masts and round the dark formidable frames of the rested ships.

My poor aching eyes smarted after the dullness of the passageways which led from my lodging and from the rising dockside stench, made worse by all manner of matter abandoned after a voyage or festering in gullies. The cats circled and sprung about, darting from underfoot, into safe haven.

Outside the alehouse, the red petticoats of the ship-women kicked up to a jig, making a pretty scene, even for them; some young ones danced around afore them with flowers stuck into their braids, looking chaste and scrubbed by contrast. Some little ones clambered onto barrels and swung on tether posts. Some loblolly rested against the wall looking as if he needed help, despite the smile on his befuddled face.

There was joy to be found here this day.

"Over here, Will," the young groom called, full of life and forgetfulness to his position. The freshness of his face, the clean linen of his shirt, sat at odds with the industry about him and the smell that continued to drift in from the holds, their wares and the packhorses that stood by. These warrens and sewers were not made for the genteel folks they presented as today; the tar and hemp made for a strange perfume.

It was of no matter to the groom this day though; he saw only love and hope as his bride stood beside him as free and as beautiful as she would ever be.

"We'll call it after the great ship!" he called, touching Lotte's belly as gently as big, rough working hands could be.

There was quite a gathering about them. Some obviously in their cups, tripping up and over the ropes as they made to dance. I could see a fair crowd come up the Bath lane. All were merry. A buxom woman, fair in her time, cheeks rosy, hair tinged bright and fighting to rid itself of her cap, carolled with a plantation man whose voice rose in his strange twang over hers in song.

I was pleased to join them and call them friend; life at sea can be lonesome despite the close quarters, and a man needs reality even if it's a port filled with fighting ships, dealers in dangerous trades and whores.

These people were decent enough and welcomed me as if I were family, just like the Orientals where I lodged and the man of letters who held my papers for me. They all expected to see me back in port when the ships came in.

"Have a cup," a tall young man greeted me and we drank to the health of the new couple in the shadows of the gallant ship of war, hailing love and liberty, calling on each to be enthusiastic in our salutations of this land and its people.

"Down with the French," came a call.

"To the happy couple!" shouted I, seeing Madame's sharp in-take of breath before she shouted, "Bonaparte!" fiercely in his face.

"To little Victor!" Will cried.

"Or Victoria!" the sweet bride called back like the little lark that she was.

"I've brandy, courtesy of our cousins abroad."

I ventured my bottle and followed on as we all entered the house by the quay where jugs of ale and a spread of food had been made ready for us, away from the pedlars and pushers and all manner of folk that thrived outside in these docklands.

And the cats still prowled.

Chapter 2

Contemporary Bristol

Vix entered, illuminated by the final glow of the receding sun behind her. She moved through the throng of customers usually expected on a Friday evening in the University Arms; small groups of colleagues, expectant couples on the threshold of a weekend and the regular loners who peppered the dark shiny bar. She breathed in past through and between them all as she peered into the dimness of the pub's interior trying to catch sight of someone she knew. She mounted a small flight of steps, which added to her stature, and could make out the familiar outline of Richard – Rix to her Vix – holding court. That was their only similarity.

As she approached, she could hear him more clearly too, that high-pitched excitable canter of a voice that matched those expressive hand movements that she had first targeted from the stairs. As she neared, his full throttled conversation ended abruptly.

"Darling," Rix turned and pulled her slight form into a tight embrace, forcing a glass of wine into her hand. "Gorgeous to see you. Love the look."

Vix stroked her unusually tidy hair, a chignon of sorts, courtesy of the trainees at the local college, glad that the low bar lights would soften the very red streak they had also talked her into – to liven up her unimpressive natural light brown, presumably.

She felt instant relief that at least she had someone to talk to. Or listen to, to be more exact. Richard could be guaranteed to entertain at this time of the evening. He had his downsides but all in all, Vix thought of him as a good mate to have. A man at her side for those occasions when she needed one, as well as someone to gossip with over coffee or at the water machine. He always knew the Department gossip and she had spent many an evening, glass of wine in one hand and the phone in the other, quite amazed at just what he knew. Or what he readily shared his opinions on, which strangely were not always necessarily true.

Richard seemed to have quite a few with him who Vix didn't recognise from work tonight; there was only the new guy Jeremy, getting increasingly close to that nice little Polish girl from Performing Arts, and the 'girls-in-black' trio who looked so earnest and clever. The others, she wasn't sure of at all. Mostly men. No change there. Vix smiled to herself, watching Richard beam and target a couple of potentials. She had got used to the behaviour of her fickle new friend.

Some, however, mainly from Finance, glanced at their watches periodically; on their way back home to suburbia, the wife, kids and takeaway, was her guess. But that was normal life, even if it wasn't hers now.

Vix surmised quite a lot about them all as she stood there looking on, amused by yet another of Richard's tales and trying to fit in.

The place seemed busier than usual. People squeezed themselves into small gaps and any passageways, got louder, more ebullient and the small flight of stairs kept creaking with the traffic of hopefuls who pushed their way up in search of seats, leaning places or somewhere to rest a drink.

"Excuse me chaps, just seen someone I might get to know," Rix announced, springing off and feeling his way through them all like the host of a party.

"I'll come Rix, need a refill."

The tall blond man by his side moved off with him, leaving Vix alone with a fixed welcoming smile just about clinging onto her face as she nodded to the little group perched on the stools, too engrossed with each other to notice.

It was hard being the new girl on the block, particularly when you were not such a 'girl' anymore. That was probably what got her involved with Dr Stanley's silly experiments. *Why did Charlie have to work in 'Para-psychology'?* Vix cringed involuntarily and sipped some more of her drink.

She thought that Charlie would meet her here tonight and hoped that she hadn't made a complete idiot of herself either. Vix knew that Charlie would tell her, she always had been brutally honest, even at school.

Vix fumbled eagerly for her mobile phone as it throbbed in her bag.

"At last," she breathed, her free hand paddling into its depths to get it as she balanced her glass and smiled down to Richard, who, for some reason, was bellowing her name before turning towards the blond.

Vix retrieved it too late, but continued to clutch it tightly and close, hoping the retry button would respond, the flagging signal ignite and she could answer it. Anything other than just stand there drinking too much cheap, warm, white wine.

Vix looked up as the noise suddenly increased; voices, deep and urgent, angry-sounding, cut through the general din of the pub. She noticed some large brutal-looking men push their way through, down below, the sparse light of the main bar, into the warren of alcoves and nooks. The suits, hair and expressions all matched. They looked like they were on a mission. They behaved like an army would have marched in and out if it had been possible; there was a bit of a stir, courtesy of the mouthy young blokes at the bar as they returned, but not for long. Their expressions silenced anything further.

"Hi, can I share your space?" Vix said, "If you wouldn't mind."

Vix eyed the man, before smiling back at him. She didn't know him.

"Rix, you mean."

"I'm Vix," she answered through the chatter and piped music.

"Yes, that's what I meant," he laughed, his eyes dark and shining, illuminated by the sidelights just above him.

"Expecting a call?" he said.

Vix realised that she still had her mobile clutched in her hand and felt herself redden.

"Yes-No, sort of, it's probably too early yet."

"1805."

Vix felt a little shiver, followed by momentary embarrassment as her mind leapt back to that afternoon's session.

"I'm Will," he announced, offering her his hand, "you're ice cold."

His voice sounded sympathetic; he was shrouded in dark, his eyes deep pools as he peered at her, he was haloed by golden wavy hair and he seemed momentarily intangible. He looked just like *him*. But he was here, now.

She guessed he noticed how uncomfortable she felt, but he stood his ground, smiling. She wasn't sure how it had happened, but here she was, standing and talking to a tall striking-looking man. She allowed herself to smile back.

"I was talking about someone called Will all afternoon," she said, trying to be bright and engaging, trying to keep him there and, more importantly, not to think about the *Will* of those strange sessions with Dr Dai Stanley.

Vix hadn't really appreciated just how traumatised she had been by the experience. Jumping at the time, and then someone's name. Whatever next?

"A great crowd," Will said, gesturing towards Richard and his little posse who were attempting a rumba to the bar for refreshments.

"Yes, they are," Vix agreed, hurriedly recounting a story or two about Rix's crowd before she knew it and allowing her phone to pulsate to its self, safely ensconced once again in the depths of her enormous bag.

***

Her answer phone flashed red when she finally turned up at home.

Vix hadn't lived in the small block for long; it was old with appliances that operated at whim and loose old bathroom taps that wobbled, but it was handy for work and cheap. It was better moving here than staying put after all that fuss and scandal, as well. They were a mixed bunch in the neighbourhood, mostly sound enough, apart from the bike boys who toppled and bounced their little wheels with a nod to confer, pick-up, go with their cargo or instructions, heels spinning into the night, out of sight. They were largely outside of Vix's experience, but she noticed them and ignored them like everyone else.

"It's me, Charlie, pick up if you're in."

Then,

"I tried the mobile, Ring me."

Finally,

"Where are you? Call me."

Vix decided to put Charlie out of her misery. Anyway, she wanted to share her excitement. It's not every day that she received an invitation from a rather interesting and good-looking man, after all. She caught herself smiling, more a mischievous little smirk, and laughed out loud again. It had been a while since she had felt this comfortable around a man. It was a while since she had felt so excited, alive even, and with the need to smile quite as much. She felt lifted. A strange thought really, when she had been speaking with the dead all afternoon.

Her life had become strange though. If someone had said to her last year that she would have been married, separated, held by the police and hounded by the media, losing her job in the bargain, she would have thought them deranged. That sort of thing didn't happen to a well brought-up privately educated middle class girl from Somerset.

Allowing Charlie to talk her into helping with the paranormal research of that Dr Dai Stanley, now seemed a serious error of judgement; or a measure of the loneliness and boredom of her life recently.

But Charlie had been kind and Vix could never resist her plans and schemes; her knowing almond eyes had helped persuade many into actions they never realised they wanted to do. It had been the same during their years together at school, and then university. Charlie could be a charmer, when she decided to.

Charlie, Charlotte, always well-attired, adored daughter of a wealthy, older foreign couple who had managed to produce a wonderful mixture of a person; wilful and loving, spontaneous and forthright, but serious when it mattered and surprisingly sensitive too, if needed.

When Charlie spoke, you could hear English Church bells, 'howzat' across the Green, the smell of Sunday lunch or afternoon tea. All of which, belied her parents sober, restrained manner and rather secretive exterior. Perhaps, things are never quite as they seem to outsiders.

Vix smiled again but less confidently and flopped into the old leather sofa, stretching herself out on its long low base and trying to recall every detail she needed for their meeting the next morning: Waterloo, 10 am, Platform 4.

She was determined not to dwell on all those 'coincidences', all could be logically explained, after all. The prospect of a wedding reception in Old Portsmouth on the Victory sounded delightful, not eerie in the slightest, particularly not when she considered the man she was going with. It was not in her nature to be frightened off.

Without hesitation, Vix reached for her phone:

"Hello, answering machine! Sorry that I can't tell you this directly Charlie, but, so, just met a guy and I'm off to a wedding with him tomorrow. Portsmouth, Victory. Night."

Just the outfit to sort out, she never was much good at fancy dress.

A cat's chorus filtered up to her from below, but she closed the window and blind to focus on the outfit. After everything she had been through, it seemed a justifiable indulgence and she meant to enjoy it – and the new guy she had met, the enigmatic Will.

Chapter 3

They gathered by her as the flags fluttered and a breeze blew up across the water. It gave the vessel a sense of movement as its great wooden body presented itself before them, flanked by the grey land made to hold her just so.

She was still noble, the richness of her golden wood made more so by the care of time and the blackened timbers that appeared to shape her elegance; she stood proud in greeting, her bell faintly sounding.

The masts tall and making still such a statement of strength, ropes descending, tied meaningfully to her sides, sails hidden, but prepared, alert. The perched canons peering from their holes and rests told you that. The decks were bare, scrubbed and ready too, the little buckets jostling each other in a line with the sound of wind and sea moving through their arms. The canopy above the steps that led below joined in with a flutter of canvas and a rock of its lamp, as the weather took on a change and the candy floss clouds turned to grey.

The Victory did not disappoint.

The wedding guests milled around, making contact with long forgotten relatives, old friends or colleagues. Most hugged and kissed and laughed. Others were more restrained, self-conscious, perhaps, in their attempts at period dress. The children played around, really entering into the spirit of the occasion with unrestrained excitement and verve, ignored by busy parents flushed by afternoon champagne. All contributed to the atmosphere; the drama of the time, the tenacity and spirit embodied in the fine ship behind them and the prospect of a good time. They were there for celebration.

Vix was unsure why Will had needed to go off so quickly, and in such eager pursuit of that guy with the heavy accent.

Will had left Vix with his drink, and two girls playing hide and seek around her full swaying skirt, to catch up with the man.

There is something going on, she surmised

"Come on, don't wait there. Come on board with us."

Vix realised that the kindly older couple were talking to her. She was about the last one left to run the gauntlet of introductions. Several couples and small groups had arrived after her, and had joined the party, in the time that she had been standing there alone and waiting for Will. She didn't want to explain that she didn't actually know any of the people she was introduced to.

They must have felt sorry for her, and somehow that irritated her even more. That and the coldness that was creeping up her voluminous skirt, and stinging her thin, bare arms that demanded a good cardigan, not a flimsy pashmina. It was a stupid choice of an outfit. She had been inspired by a picture in a book, sort of Vivienne Westward, but not quite. It sort of reminded her of those characters she had been asked to describe by Dai Stanley. Although she had felt sure they were just subliminal images from period TV dramas, he had been impressed.

"I'll just give him a minute," she smiled despite herself.

Thankfully, they didn't try any more to persuade. She must have seemed miserable.

"Cheers," she muttered as the waiter collected glasses for his tray, eyeing her with his bored eyes, his disinterest in her obvious.

She tried not to well up, which she thought she just might be in danger of doing, before suddenly noticing that everyone else had gone. Vix felt inexplicably lonely, not just alone, as well as bloody furious with that man, Will. He had chosen to abandon her. Ash flashed through her mind; he had been too good to be true as well and she reminded herself how that had ended. Vix didn't know who to despise more, them or herself. Her body flexed, stay or go? Even that decision eluded her today.

The choice to stay or go was finally made by the rain.

As Vix left, she ran across the old paving slabs and cobbles, oblivious to the old metal tracks she caught her heels in and the small stumpy bollards that broke her fall on more than one occasion.

She felt ashamed, and once again used by a man.

Vix managed to navigate her way out of the old dockyards to find a way back to her hotel. But not until she had suffered the final indignity of actually seeing Will again.

He had been running down the main road and towards the station or ferryboats. Perhaps, she was sure that he must have seen her as she shouted at him; those around her most certainly stopped, especially as she stamped her feet.

He seemed to be running after someone, or being chased, with a posse of young boys darting around, trying to get ahead or out of the way; they certainly had completely disappeared when she looked again.

As she turned the corner, she heard voices and one was clearly his.

'Victory' is what it had sounded like. Perhaps, he was on his way back?

Then nothing. He was gone, vanished, in a screen of people and cars. She was left with just this maelstrom and the long journey home alone.

"No, you can't come I'm afraid," Vix said to the ginger cat that folded itself between her ankles and snaked about her feet. It was the first real smile she had experienced all day.

Chapter 4

Richard Rich walked purposefully towards work. He couldn't think up another 'Monday morning story' without wincing, momentarily embarrassing even himself. The last excuse had been a neighbour having a heart attack he thought, or that was possibly the time before when he'd ended up in Brighton for the weekend and had to catch the milk train back. But it had been a good weekend. That was when he had met Danny. *Never mind*, he thought with a whimsical smile, *some things and all that...*

Richard's life had turned out to be a catalogue of nearly but not quite adventures in an attempt to find 'Mr Right' or possibly to avoid facing his reality: he was nearly 40 years old, had a low-paying, sort-of-interesting sounding job in the Arts Faculty and was going bald. Thank God he could work the look and the jaw kept its line in place; the thought of that sagging was too much. The fact that he could have been better qualified, an academic if he had tried to, or an art producer, or indeed anything other than a really, very ordinary senior administrator in a below-par department; all that had been pushed from his radar years ago.

Richard had really wanted to be an actor. If only his good bone structure and manly shoulders hadn't been let down by his rather short legs, it led to disappointment when he stood up, particularly on first meetings.

It didn't stop him indulging occasionally in some little productions and as was generally agreed, he could always be called upon for theatrics.

A cyclist turning the corner cut across Richard's path and returned his expletive with a 'V' sign and a smile.

"Bloody bikes," Richard mouthed to himself as he crossed the side road.

He had considered texting Vix on the off chance, to see if she had left yet; it would be better to walk in with someone.

He noticed the police car outside her block and although it intrigued him, could even have been another 'Monday morning-er', he thought it better to get on. He'd had a messy weekend and couldn't really cope with it. So, he carried on up the road, turning up the collar of his rain-mac, feeling the chill as the early morning sun disappeared and a wind blew up.

It would be reasonable, he pondered, *to be a little late if you were concerned about a colleague,* quickly texting Vix before throwing his phone into his satchel with a smile.

They had arrived early, too early, it was work time and all those who passed Vix's door could see the police knocking. A uniformed man and woman, both quite young; the policeman appeared almost bored, disinterested, by his assigned task. Not so the woman police officer. She was eager and direct. No gently, gently with her as she stood, feet firmly planted, shoulders back, outside Vix's front door.

"How can I help?"

Vix heard herself say in a tone that she would not have directly attributed to herself these days, something leftover from school perhaps, when faced with authority or something. Whatever, she was uncomfortable with it.

She had been slow to answer the door in an effort to be presentable. As she let them in, her eyes followed theirs over the opened suitcase, a discarded supper clinging to the plate and a pile of clothes from Friday night. The room looked generally a mess of piled books, half-drunken coffee from stained mugs and too many possessions in a small space.

Vix pulled open the blinds in an attempt to brighten things up, normalise them. She turned to smile at the police and gestured they could sit. They preferred not to.

"We would like to know your whereabouts this weekend."

"Me? Mine?" Her throat felt dry. "Well, I was here on Friday, left on Saturday to go to a wedding reception in Portsmouth," Vix gabbled. She reimagined herself being interrogated all over again. Saw the photo of Ash they had slapped before her.

They seemed to like what she said and Vix was happy to continue with train times, hotel reservations, wedding venue, in fact, more than she realised she knew came out and she kept going.

“You say you do not know the name of the man you went with though,” it was a statement from the policeman, somehow now motivated to speak.

“Will, his name was Will. We’d only just met.” Vix read the pair’s expression. “Look, I don’t make a habit of this sort of thing you know.”

They continued to nod and stare. *Perhaps, this is their way of being non-judgemental*, Vix thought, wishing she had put more clothes on, *trousers would have been good*, she reflected, even with the long top she had grabbed.

“Look, why are you asking all this?” she finally rallied in her fight to gain a little ground in what seemed to be turning into an inquisition. She had regretted not asserting herself last time. “What has all this got to do with me?” she almost demanded as she walked off to claim her jeans after all.

Her mouth felt dry and she felt flushed now too. Finishing the bottle of red and not really eating hadn’t helped; she felt terrible. A quick glance in the bedroom mirror confirmed red-rimmed eyes to match the hanging red-streak of hair that fell over her mottled face, strangely almost yellow and pink, where it wasn’t grey with redundant mascara. She began to question herself, wonder if anything had actually happened, something she didn’t want to admit even to herself.

“We have to tell you that your information is important to us because there is a crime scene investigation in that area of Old Portsmouth, by the Victory, where you were a guest at a wedding. Luckily, you were easy to trace from your hotel booking as you were the only unknown person according to the others we have interviewed. The man you were with seems a bit of a mystery.”

The policeman was suddenly more talkative, the lethargy of earlier had left him, and the woman became quiet. *Was this how they operated?* Vix had to learn not to trust anyone.

“A man has disappeared from the wedding family and now another man, who we believe could have been your companion, has been reported as also possibly missing, by his girlfriend.”

Vix tried not to look shocked, well, not shocked at the girlfriend bit. After all, the disappearance of two people was more important than being jilted or two-timed. But she had seen the look in that policeman's face and noted that intonation in his voice. She felt ridiculous.

"We need to see if there is any connection. You might help us make one."

Vix listened as they continued to make her aware of the importance of any information she may have, of the distress caused to the bride in particular and the family generally, including the missing man's young son.

Why hadn't she known more about the man? This Will, she had consented to go away with. If only she could have told them more, understood what all this was about. She felt a little dizzy, wondered if she was actually listening to them, *Why did names like Rose, Percy and George sting her memory when she just didn't know of them? How does she explain any of it to them*, she asked herself. She did not want to be ridiculed further.

Vix's phone sounded: a text. She cast her eyes to it before walking across the room to show the police out. The tiny hall way prevented her opening the door for them but she followed close behind the pair to make sure the door was slammed closed and then locked.

It had all started to trouble her again. Had they asked her to the police station? They had last time. She had been forced to attend, to go to identify him, her new husband, a man she didn't obviously really know; an illegal who had married her only to incriminate her. Love and marriage didn't necessarily go together when there were bigger causes at stake. She was just collateral damage, was that what they said? No wonder they now seemed to expect her to be involved somehow, it seemed practically automatic; Victoria and the disappearing men.

She shuddered.

"OMG. What's with the fuzz outside yours??? Rix" the text read.

But how had this all happened, was all that kept going round in her mind.

She decided to give Rix the basic details at first, before being edged on by his usual probing, his turns of phrase that elicited more than you ever wanted to say. But at least she could tell someone who might just believe her.

Vix finally read:

"Nothing to do with me – DO NOT know him."

He was gone after that and Vix sat wondering how she could have thought otherwise and that Will would automatically have been one of Rix's friends. It was a pub for Christ's sake! It had seemed so clear at the time. This Will *had* spoken to, and of, Rix, after all, surely, she had seen him herself and he knew his name, he…perhaps, there was a different explanation. A different reality began to dawn on Vix. The noise, the bustle and jostle of loud lively people had obscured how things really were. It was hard to feel so wrong.

Chapter 5

Dr Dai Stanley had a certain charm, particularly for older women. He wasn't conventionally good-looking, but dressed well and was always attentive. He paid great attention to detail, even being known to have patterned ties that matched his socks, if only in tone, or silk handkerchiefs had been known on occasion. The ginger hair of his youth had become fashionably subdued. He even quite liked it now. The sadness for Dai was that he was unable to recognise that his appeal, despite such thought and detail, did not extend to the younger women who he came into contact with. Things were not as they once were, was a familiar incantation to himself nowadays.

His lilting Welsh tones held less appeal when his hands stayed too long where they were not invited. His proximity had been known to offend a few of the young women who had worked for him over the years. However, nothing was ever really said. Dr Dai was generally liked. No need for fuss. Some of his male colleagues thought there was too much of that these days anyway.

Charlie actually liked him. He somehow didn't do any of those things, things that offended the others, to her and they enjoyed a relationship of banter and teasing that somehow held itself within the bounds of acceptability. He also knew her father. They shared a past apparently, but that was never discussed.

"Hi, Vix. He wants you to undergo another regression. Later."

Charlie left a message on Vix's answer phone in her clear bubbly tones. She would pick it up on her return from Portsmouth and no doubt call with the gossip. She would find out things she was sure.

"I'll drop over with the transcript for you," she finished.

It was unfortunate timing. Vix was not in any mood to talk to, let alone reason with and certainly had nothing for them to laugh about. *Best keep it short and sweet*, thought Charlie, congratulating herself on her sensitivity.

"She doesn't want to do it," Charlie informed a rather staid Dai Stanley on Monday morning.

His reaction surprised Charlie, until she looked at him.

It was cold, dull and grey and the usually exuberant Dr Dai matched it. His glasses rested so low on his nose that they only remained there with cunning, seizing the flare of his nostrils before his nose came to an abrupt end.

Vix's reaction was understandable, Charlie considered, particularly after that shoddy treatment by the dream man, Will. She realised she shouldn't, but Charlie allowed herself a little smirk. It had seemed too good to be true; a tall good-looking fella with devilish dark eyes and all that confidant hair whisking her off for the weekend within a couple of hours of meeting, and no morning after. What nerve, the man had!

Vix was a magnet for trouble where men were concerned. Charlie still couldn't quite work out why Vix had taken up with that student; he wasn't even that good-looking, too thin, too quiet and he didn't have any money. If she had listened to her friend she wouldn't have gone out with him in the first place, let alone marry the guy. Vix was too trusting. Charlie made a mental note to talk to her, gently, about this 'Will' character, when they met. She needed to protect her.

"Good weekend?" she queered with a smile, reading the look on Dai's face and burying hers into her screen again. She noted his eyes seemed more hooded than usual and his fair skin was turning blotchy with the warmth of the room. He was decidedly sorry for himself. Even a screensaver of a lush green hilltop complete with serene looking yoga types, delicate wispy clouds and an ethereal vista beyond, didn't distract from the poor pathetic specimen that Dai Stanley was today.

Eventually, she thought she ought to go to get some coffee, which seemed to appeal because he smiled back in what could only be taken for gratitude.

"Thanks, sweety," Dai uttered lifelessly as Charlie left.

As Charlie placed the Americanos down, she told a slightly more open-eyed Dai Stanley that Vix had changed her mind; she *would* do it again, having read the transcript of her regression, but it had to be very soon.

"Well done," Dai said, although Charlie wasn't sure if he meant her, Vix or the coffee. But it was good coffee.

"Apparently, it's of more interest now, after an incident at the weekend."

He looked mildly interested as Charlie spoke.

"Yes, she went to Portsmouth and some guy called William invited her to a wedding reception on the Victory. Spooky." Charlie smiled in her child-like mischievous manner, sipping away at the cooling coffee and telling him more. It seemed to restore him, he was even surprisingly interested.

"You look a bit better now," Charlie gave a satisfied shrug as she put down her large paper mug, noticing a defensive look from Dai before moving off.

"So many colds about at the minute, change of weather probably."

She continued to mouth across the room, although she couldn't stop her golden-green cat eyes from shining, which contradicted the look of sincerity she wanted to convey. She gave herself away. She was trained to do better.

"Yes, well, I'm absolutely fine. I'll take your friends details again now, if I may. I want to let her know my plans for the next session."

Charlie smiled. Dai seemed to be back on form, although still a little quiet.

Vix couldn't wait for Charlie to meet her that evening; having faced the police and everyone at work was one thing, but the stuff Charlie had sent to her was crazy. She needed to talk about it to someone.

"Are you telling me?"

"Yes," Vix interjected, "the man in the regression is also called Will, I keep remembering names from the reception that are here in this transcript as well, let alone the venue, the event. I could *not* have known all that detail about a place I'd never been to or such times, Charlie. You know me and history from school."

"OK, OK. Don't get so excited; they're looking over at us, you'll frighten them."

"Actually, Charlie I feel a little bit 'mad', if that's what you are going to say."

Vix peered at the couple on the next table who hurriedly looked into their food, and immediately hated herself.

"Anything else?" Charlie enquired hesitantly.

"Lots of silly things, coincidences I suppose, but really unsettling, like the men who had marched into and right through the pub, you know, when I first met my Will."

Vix noted Charlie's raised eyebrow but continued.

"As opposed to the one on paper, here." She held the transcript up and smiled, this time to the couple near them as her eyes caught their interested gaze once again. She lowered her tone.

"All too similar to those guards, or whatever they were, who came after this other Will."

"Similar, you're right, but not necessarily the same," Charlie reasoned.

"Look, it just strikes me as…well, something I can't just ignore."

"OK, let's change the subject."

Vix knew that tone and complied, although noting that Charlie was getting over-controlling these days.

They relaxed into the high-backed chairs by the wood-effect log burner of the snug bar and Charlie tried to entertain Vix with gossip. She was expert at various character assassinations, especially of some of the people in her department, particularly Dr Stanley. She was good at directing people.

Both knew that what they really wanted to talk about was Will, the one on paper as well as the one Vix had met in the flesh. Where had he gone? What made him behave like that? Why me, was what rattled at Vix.

"Hello, girls," Rix had entered on his own, quietly and looking very neat, almost proper, for him.

"He's probably meeting someone," Charlie quickly whispered to Vix as he crossed towards them.

"Can't stop," he announced as they looked up at him with welcoming expectant smiles.

They wouldn't have minded his company tonight, went through both their minds, at least he would distract them from thinking about Will.

“Meeting Mother,” he said, before disappearing off into another area marked: ‘Food Kitchen’ in large green letters, looking very contemporary and discerning.

“Well, even Rix has a mother I suppose,” Charlie chirped.

“Wonders.”

Vix and Charlie laughed and waved to Rix as he took his mother’s arm into the restaurant. They looked like doubles.

“You see, I thought Will knew Rix,” Vix said with renewed determination.

“I’ll get us another drink,” Charlie went to the bar with resignation on her face.

Vix has been through it, after all, she thought, but she didn’t want her dwelling on it or digging too deeply. This needed her to control it.

“Guess what, Charlie,” Vix called out, standing up by her chair with a huge smile she didn’t try to conceal.

”I’ve just received a text from Will, he wants to meet up and explain. Look.”

“Bastard,” Charlie said, grabbing the mobile from Vix’s shaking hands to see for herself.

Chapter 6

They got merry; more folk gathered and the early evening light sat softly on them as they rolled around, loving one and all and calling each a brother indeed no matter the connection or length of acquaintance. The house we celebrated in was presentable enough to us all and the bow of the window gave view of England's glory: her navy. The songs were bawdy, as only sailors and these dockside sorts knew, but wrapped us up well in laughter, an indulgence I hadn't known for a while.

An old couple consoled a young thin woman with red hair who seemed to be abandoned by the quayside, her small tear-stained face made for a sad sight on such an evening as this. It made no difference to the young ones who played about her mind; they were ever hopeful to steal some of the gin placed down to partake in a kick or two on the cobbles, before they were shoed off, to give any mind to her.

I could see some of the Jacks, not content with matters, posturing along the dockside, pigtails swaying vigorously as they went in close and darted back again from some old Turtlebacks. They turned as some young lads came by, shouting news of some sorts. The faces through the window suddenly looked fierce and troubled, all laughter and banter ceased, dancing, music too, as they raced from group to group, crossing over the dockside towards the house.

"Will!" went up the shout.

"Will, get thee gone."

Inside the house, all faded and died to a silence. Outside the cobbles rung with the sound of feet, fleeing feet and heavy, determined marching feet gaining quickly behind.

The woman started first and then the girls, shrill cries and shrieks of horror, of knowing. The young bride stood still, then collapsed and sobbed without control. Some ran out. Their youth and vigour prompting fearless calls, rough insults and the throwing of stones, or anything that came to hand, all directed with the skill of the sharp-eyed at the gang after their men.

"They'll get 'em," some others called out, rushing to close and bar the door.

"We'll see about that," the one called Sarah cried as she ran out as they went to push it shut.

"Close the shutters," an old timer called to those left and not comforting poor Lotte in her grief.

"I've seen these blagg'rds 'efore. They'll take 'em, they'll not been seen again in a good while," he went on, looking down into his tankard.

"If at all," Madame ventured as she eyed the warships.

Outside, the calls and screams continued to chill us. I should have done something; I just stood and waited, left them to it. I should have, but I didn't.

***

Vix stood quietly at the bar by the window in the suggested coffee shop, 'Caprice', trying to smile lightly as she leaned against the high upholstered stool, fearful of actually sitting on it; she didn't want to attract any attention or comments. She just wanted to be ready, poised if she could manage it, for when Will arrived. She had planned what she wanted to say.

Naturally, he would not expect her to be gushing and excited to see him again. He'd been in the wrong after all. But Vix figured, her acceptance of his invitation to meet meant she wouldn't be hostile exactly either. She needed to get the right balance. But she needed to be in control and make sure he understood how she had felt. Perhaps, even why.

"Hello there,"

Vix turned, a smile forming uncontrollably on her face, sweeping her eyes up slowly to meet his. Automatic suddenly took control. She reined in the smile and let her wide eyes settle back to a steadier, almost distracted, glance.

"I thought that was you. Looking very pretty today, may I say. Green suits you. Red and green, my favourite colours," Dai Stanley continued as he stood smiling broadly at Vix, who tried desperately not to show her complete bitter disappointment; the sort that makes you sick.

She heard herself say things:

"Hello,

"Yes, he could join her,

"No, she wasn't planning on staying long,

"Yes, perhaps just a small coffee."

How could this have happened? shot through her head.

Vix scanned the road outside, then the tables around her every time she heard a chair scrape, the entrance each time the door pushed in with a sweep. Each male voice was tuned into as they approached.

The appointed hour had come and gone, and there was no Will. Just this dreadful leach of a man, Stanley. Vix wanted to cry, then scream with frustration, then explode with anger.

"Your friend obviously couldn't make it," Dai Stanley said with what looked like a subdued smile to Vix.

She reprimanded herself. It wasn't right to turn her anger on Stanley. She tried to look interested in what he was saying, even smiled a little to compensate momentarily, before the effort was too much, her thoughts just kept drifting elsewhere. Will.

"No; not a firm arrangement," Vix said, archly, forgetting to be nice, before indicating that he should go on.

"I'd very much like you to come over to my place."

Dai laughed again and raised his eyebrows, patting her hands as they sat in her lap, removing them swiftly as she straightened and fixed him with a glare.

He was practised at knowing when to rein himself in, Vix thought, and his actions were certainly timely given her mood at this moment.

"I'm having a showing of the research findings, your regression, please do come along. It could be very enlightening for the research team as well as for yourself, of course."

He continued pleasantly, ignoring her frosty response.

"Possibly."

Vix was anxious not to appear too interested, in case he thought that she might just be interested in him. She didn't understand fully how she'd got herself into this situation. She had never intended getting involved with a man again so soon and had never wanted to do the regression, and yet, here she was doing both and actually now wanting both. The similarities, coincidences, call them what you will, didn't stop bombarding her thoughts. The compelling idea of Will kept resurfacing. The attractive, interesting and now so undoubtedly, git of a man, Will, was never far from her thoughts. Vix kept returning to the manuscripts she had read and going over again and again her meeting with Will, and the vivid impression that she had had of knowing the Victory and of knowing him.

She had to learn more. That might be better, channelling her thoughts into that, than dealing with the hurt and anger of being stood up by the bloke.

"Perhaps, Charlie could let me have the details, we could go together, I'd feel safer."

Vix's tone was even and controlled but Dai Stanley would have seen the strength of her look and noted its message.

"Of course," he said, running his hands through his hair.

Chapter 7

"Please, sit down," this time it was the Inspector and he insisted, "you need to listen carefully."

Vix could see that he meant business; there was a new determination in his voice and she complied without another thought. He was drab; the cropped light hair, the dull grey eyes and the pallor of his skin, all unremarkable. The smell of tobacco and coffee his only significant features, apart from his inquisitorial stare and the notebook, hallmarks of his trade.

He spoke without actually looking at her, "We have discovered that your friend, Williams, was leading a double life, this was only one of his addresses it seems."

He then scanned her for a response.

"Look, and I do keep saying this, I only met William twice, here in Bristol and we went to Portsmouth for the wedding reception the next day. He has nothing more to do with me than that. We met and he just asked me out. End of story."

Vix stared back at him, although she could not maintain it, she lacked his training. He had her there.

"Not quite so," she saw him smirk. "Williams regularly came to Bristol and was seen in this very building. A bit of a coincidence, wouldn't you think? Then you were both in Portsmouth, together, according to the hotel. There is a crime scene and a missing person. I'm not getting much of a response. Strange, wouldn't you say?"

"No," Vix almost shrieked this time. Then, "He was not visiting me," spoken with determined calmness, "when he was seen here; I only met him the twice."

The Inspector merely turned to his colleague, who leaned against the wall in a state of permanent resignation. He merely raised one brow and adjusted his pose slightly every so often.

"You need to know that we will be liaising with our colleagues on the south coast and that we would appreciate you being in touch, if you do hear from him. He's a very dangerous man. If you're not aware of what he does, as you say, then you could be in danger too. Nice girls should steer clear."

"What do you mean? What does he do?"

The two men looked at each other, as if assessing her naivety on some sort of scale. She must have registered high for gullibility.

"He's a drugs smuggler, basically. That and people. Small fry really but nonetheless, we need to get to him to get to others. Bigger fish, you might say. Not your sort of person usually, I'd guess? Although, who can tell these days."

The Inspector stopped peering at her, nodded to his colleague and with that they made to leave.

"Do you really think that I'm involved? Like the last time, eh? When I was a terrorist, or someone happy to assist one?" Vix felt herself redden in the face, felt the anger rise. That experience with Ash had been torment and she couldn't go through that again.

"We aren't pursuing that angle."

So, he does have a voice, she thought. *Good cop, bad cop routine?*

"Be careful and let us know anything you can about his whereabouts. Here's my card, although you probably won't need it, if my hunch is correct, he's already dead."

Chapter 8

The room was small and had been set out like a small theatre of sorts, the chairs in three semi-circular rows with a large white screen for the audience.

The tall ceilings of the room, its large windows and wooden floors sent out an echo as Vix walked over to Charlie, who waved cheerily from her seat at the front.

The pictures on the walls, old incumbents of the place most like, looked down austerely and Vix noted their self-assurance, the total belief in themselves and why they deserved such homage, as their eyes traced her as she walked forward. She wanted some of that herself right now, a shot of arrogance in the arm would do nicely.

A few people, more than she had hoped, or expected, peppered the seats and chatted lightly as they waited. Vix didn't know any of them, which was a real relief. Apart from Dai Stanley, of course, who smiled broadly at her as she approached. Ordinarily she would have returned his gesture out of sheer politeness, but the policeman's remarks haunted her. All this stuff suddenly seemed so trite compared to someone dealing in smuggling drugs, people and who knows what. According to them, Will was very possibly dead, with herself now in actual danger.

She had heard from him and had not said a word, she had the email to prove it. Vix did not recognise herself. No wonder she gulped, had sweaty palms and felt dizzy.

It was just so difficult to reconcile it all in her mind. She could not make sense of what was happening, nor of the coincidences that seem to have bound them, her and this Will, which this regrettable regression back in time just kept reinforcing. More than that, it drove her, to find out more, to understand, to get him to explain. She felt compelled.

"Thank you all for coming," Dai Stanley opened proceedings. He introduced the project team, those researching the paranormal, the parapsychologists, the mediums from various organisations, their press and a couple of sceptics for the sake of balance. Although both 'balances' seemed quite young, pretty and enjoying his attention. They also didn't seem to know why they were there.

"I will run the recording and then we can have a discussion after that. I'm sure the team will be happy to take questions."

Dai's smile was, as usual, full, and ended with a sudden clamping of lips that pumped up his cheeks and rendered his eyes almost invisible.

"We have the absolute pleasure of having with us this evening, Victoria, who took part in the regression for us."

Vix notably coloured as eyes fell upon her. She was thankful that Charlie had sat at the front and to the side, in case she decided to leave and in the hope she might not be fully seen. After her previous notoriety due to Ash's terrorism, she knew the importance of not being too recognisable. She didn't want to move on again.

"I'm looking forward to this," Charlie said as she popped a mint into her mouth.

"Want one?" she asked as the lights dimmed a little.

Vix slipped into the orange plastic chair, eyes fixed on the screen, the smell of mints and Dai Stanley's heavy cologne, a strange mix, as he wedged himself very closely next to her on the other side.

***

"Help me."

It was the girl with the red hair who stood on her own beside the dock, tears now ceased, screaming for someone. She had waited most of the day, an onlooker to the celebration who the others paid no mind to. She stood out. She was alone and didn't join in, even with the civilities and goodwill of some of the less rowdy guests. She seemed to shun even them.

"Run," the call from the top window echoed out.

"Run for your lives," came the cry from the side alleys that snaked up from the quay.

I could hear all those screams, see the anguish on the young faces as they passed; the hoarse cries of the men as they ran from the press gang pounded my ears like canon fire.

But I did nothing from my place by the half-shuttered window, just peered through where I could and cursed the free-flow of alcohol that robbed the men of their speed this evening.

The running seemed in vein to me as the broad, determined gang men went after them, undeterred by thought or reason, or at least not that belonging to a man of conscience.

Who would want to rob a bride of her husband on their wedding day? Who would grab a girl and fling her down like cargo?

Only he that was paid well, in kind or promises, to do so without a questioning word, bid by the navy to do their dirty work.

A navy wanting men to fight, aye, right enough, would say some men.

I'm not a radical man, but I think on the question of a navy full of men with no taste for fighting, a crew full of men wronged. I would not like to serve on such a vessel for long.

Why fight for liberty when your own is taken? That's what I would hear by rights below deck. What would Frenchy say to that? What would many an Englishman say if he knew?

They should jump in a post-chaise and visit such a port as this before they write their pamphlets. That's my own way of thinking. And a hope for speed in the fight. No, it would not do to be at sea over-long.

Thoughts are all I can offer up to this sad scene now. I'm no longer a free man myself it seems, getting too old and too fearful. I've made myself a prisoner.

"Will," she keeps calling at my side, the young abandoned bride, her simple proud finery now ruined. My heart, such as it is now, aches for her loss with her.

The four-rig Man-o-War towers over us, even moored out there in the Solent; she is needy of crew and her dogs of war were set to go hunting our way.

"Will!" she screams…

***

Vix rushed out. She could never, ever, have imagined anything like this. Seeing herself, in repose, lying on Dai Stanley's couch, talking, and through the voice of a man. Speaking of that strange other world that she had known nothing of, as if she were actually there, hardwired somehow. Talking of Will, crying out for Will. That anguish at the inability to help him. She felt sick.

She had now seen herself truly inhabit that world, and it frightened her. It sounded so plausible. So real yet so unreal. Could she really have known those times?

Vix felt at that moment that perhaps she really did know them, she certainly felt them, sensed them. But how could that be? She held her head. Had it been her laying there? She had certainly spoken, although not with her own voice. She had seen herself perspire, had witnessed her heavy breathing and fearful gasps, the twists and turns of her body. Seen the anguish in her own face.

She had been there, if only in her mind. Perhaps even in reality, just a different reality, was that it? Could she leave it at that?

Vix walked off suddenly, feeling cold and uncomfortable, blinking her eyes open; was she dreaming and was even now walking in her sleep?

She needed an explanation. Her rational sense seemed to have completely deserted her. Her head spun with conjecture.

Vix saw him clearly; Will was being pursued by a gang of men, chasing him, gaining on him, pushing others around indiscriminately as they went.

It was all so very close to what she had actually stood and witnessed, when the Will of her reality, the one she had spoken to, known, touched, had fled as those men had chased him down the street. Vix gasped as she suddenly recalled the men in the pub the night she had met Will. They must have been after him then as well. Was that it? Was she mixing up these distinct realities and merging them into an altogether different consciousness?

She mentally pinched herself before holding her head again, with both hands this time.

"What is happening to me!" she screamed.

Vix only realised what she was doing as Charlie grabbed her arm and spun her round to face her.

"Vix, stop it, stop it now; it's me, it's OK."

Charlie put an arm about her shoulders as Vix struggled to stifle her sobs.

"Will," she said

"Vix, listen, they are not the same person."

Vix stopped and looked at Charlie in amazement.

"Of course, they can't be. I get it, I know that. It's just that I cannot explain it all. It doesn't make sense. Does it?"

Vix's eyes pleaded for something that Charlie just could not respond to. She was thinking of going and giving Dai Stanley a piece of her mind later. He must have contrived something, although she couldn't think what or how. Why else would all this happen if not. Charlie didn't believe in coincidences. Particularly when she knew how free she had been with Vix's story. And she couldn't tell her friend that, but then there was much she couldn't tell her.

"Let me get you home," Charlie said, leading Vix along the corridor and outside into the light and normality of the early evening street reassuringly full of commuters, the noise of traffic and normality.

"I do need to understand all this."

"Yes, I know, of course, later we'll."

"No," Vix interrupted as she stopped dead at the corner of the street, "what you don't know is that the police have been to see me, question me."

"And?" Charlie's voice was hesitant, although her eyes begged to know more, even if they also appeared terrified at the thought. She regained herself and smiled for Vix to continue.

"Apparently, Will is a very dangerous person. Drugs, and more, they said, people trafficking. They also said he might be dead by now… And."

"And what?" Charlie said, stepping back slightly and peering at her friend as only she could, expecting to be obeyed, acting as if her own life depended on it.

Vix stayed momentarily quiet under Charlie's integrative stare.

"And I might be in danger too."

Chapter 9

The police station was a 1950s building which emulated some grandiose style of a former age, formal concrete columns and ugly grey brick. At the public entrance was an entry phone with a hastily placed notice stuck above it: 'Out of Use due to Vandalism.'

Vix allowed herself a smile of sorts before she navigated her way through the outer doors and knocked, hesitantly at first, to catch some ones attention so that she could get in, especially since she had now made her decision to speak to the Inspector.

"There you go love."

A young man with cropped patchy hair and a puffed-out jacket smiled lightly as he passed her on exiting. His face was drawn and his eyes didn't focus on Vix. She noticed his lean stained blunted fingers as he pushed the door, and his ease at being there. The police station she guessed was known territory to him, whilst she was left feeling completely phased by the place, which surprised her. It wasn't exactly her first experience of them.

"Winkleman, Inspector Winkleman," the desk attendant corrected her without humour.

She was large and frosty and Vix decided not to smile, just nod her head and follow the pointed finger to where she was supposed to sit and wait.

They made people wait, she reasoned, *sitting there. All part of the psychology*, she supposed. It added to her paranoia. That, and knowingly being watched on CCTV.

It was not meant to be a comfortable place.

The waiting area had mirror-fronted doors that led to the custody suite, reflecting the steady stream of clients. Every movement behind the façade seemed to shake it, building up a kind of tension around those who sat waiting and watching expectantly. With each tremble heads turned, then looked away.

The time ticked slowly by as Vix twisted on one of the benches amongst a disparate collection of people. Some fiddled with mobiles as they came and went, one man leapt up periodically and grunted with vexation, some seemed so familiar with the situation and committed bored resignation, one almost slept.

An older woman just kept looking straight ahead, as if not to acknowledge that she was actually there at all.

Probably lost a cat or found a wallet, Vix mused, her eye returning to the desk, noticing how some approached with naivety, as she had herself, others with temerity, but most with ease. She was clearly outnumbered.

She noted a couple of professionals, a social worker, probably, in jeans, and a solicitor in a dark suit; an interpreter or advocate or two by the look of things as well. A couple of parents escorted their truculent looking son out with nods of gratitude, or fear, to the presiding officer.

Vix stopped herself categorising them, as she found herself being stared at too. They just as surely wondered why she was there for as well. They might have been surprised went through her head. She certainly was. Or was this her now?

"Shouldn't be too long."

It was the younger policeman she had seen before. Vix nodded and looked down. She pondered on the dirt tracks in the grey striped mat, unevenly worn, *Shoddy in-keeping*, she thought. The carpet beneath was neither grey nor blue fully now, but fluff speckled, with debris blown in and scattered upon it, now just indiscriminately mottled.

Allowing her eyes to move up just slightly Vix saw the flecked wall covering curled and peeled at its joints. She felt sordid.

A victim, again.

"This way please, follow me, it's a bit of a walk."

The policeman said flatly as Vix followed him obediently through, stepping behind the mirrored doors at last. They closed firmly shut behind her. She kept up with him as he walked her through the warrens of offices, interview rooms and the like, the secured doors and notices catching her eye.

'Do not ask WHY. Do a DNA Test. Ask – WHY NOT'. One in bold red lettering on a shiny black surface read.

"Take a seat," he said eventually as they reached Winkleman's room. "I understand you have some information for us."

It was the Inspector's flat dull tone.

Vix sat and with as much clarity as she had rehearsed started to tell him what she knew: Will is alive; he had emailed her and asked to meet. She repeated her story about their brief acquaintance. She told of her regression experiences, the transcripts and the screening that she had witnessed. She went on to try and cover all the coincidences that had occurred during that experience, especially about the men pursing Will. All the things she supposed would be of interest and relevance to them. Winkleman continued with his dead stare throughout.

Vix just kept going and was even pleased with herself for keeping to her mind script, her clarity and succinctness surprised her. But she felt it, it was real. Then she saw his look.

Vix turned from him to his colleague and back again, reading Winkleman's expression. She felt flushed, she felt her throat go dry, but more than that she felt overwhelmingly ridiculous all over again.

"What part of this is not working for you?" she suddenly blurted out, as the inspector fiddled with his pen.

"Listen. All that stuff, well, it may well be all very, well, plausible, to you."

He searched for that word, Vix thought.

"But, you know, we don't, can't, deal with the supernatural. We are after a nowadays villain, that's all. We need real hard facts, things we can see, real stuff."

Vix merely looked at him. She couldn't even feel angry. She understood his reaction, if she were honest, more than her own. Last year, she may well have thought the same.

As she left he walked with her, but said little.

"Look, maybe you could let us have that email address sometime, especially if he contacts you again – in this world, that is."

Vix turned from his disinterest, his palpable ridicule if she was honest; she noted his wink to his lacklustre colleague by the doors as she exited.

She needed to go home, be alone, and think.

Chapter 10

Rix always hummed to himself as he wound up the day. It was a habit from childhood, he thought; all that busying-about with Mother. Saturdays were often spent doing the rounds of flee-markets and bric-a-brac places, as they searched for that certain something, to set off the recess in the dining room perhaps, or the telephone table in the narrow hallway, already laden with a collection of pottery animals that kept toppling over and a crinoline lady lamp that flickered.

Any such expeditions were always followed by the almost ceremonial unwrapping of their new treasures, placed one by one on the kitchen table before Rix got busy with the soapsuds and dusters.

The kitchen just couldn't have enough ill-matching crockery, either, he always reflected, as if by instinct. Rix wished that his mother had hit on a style he liked, at least he could disperse some of the hoard in his own direction, and the cupboards could heave a sigh of relief. His minimalist approach couldn't tolerate any of it, *Nowadays though*, he mused, *it almost brought on a panic attack.*

Rix sighed briefly, "If only she had one style and kept to it," he kept muttering as he worked. He had long since got used to the exchanged glances of some of those neighbours and the like, who had popped in for tea. Cabbage roses in delicate pinks clashed unfashionably with bold geometrics, even for them. But now things were getting out of hand, he decided.

It made Rix shudder just a bit. Although he comforted himself with the knowledge that she had calmed down a bit with age and he never ceased to be proud of his mother's enthusiasm for all things, if not her taste. All those hobbies and interests, the latest chums with stories to tell and a musical or two to reminisce over.

Rix did the honours and went with her to some of those and she would stand him dinner as well, a sort of reward for those regular clear-outs of her abandoned treasures for her. They went to some good cause or another, after all.

Rix secretly wondered if she ever bought them back again. She loved a charity shop.

He was good-humoured when it came to Mother, although he chose his moments when visiting her. She understood that he suffered with his nerves sometimes. And some of those 'Chums' are men and not to be encouraged. He had perfected the art of scaring them off long ago.

He enjoyed the occasional cosy night in with her in that snug flat that had been his childhood home. He knew he'd have to have a bit of a tidy and scrub-up for her first, but he'd been used to that since he could remember.

"Life is too short for hovering," she often used to say.

He guessed dusting and wiping down the kitchen surfaces were also included in that.

"Haven't you heard of bleach, Mother," she would regularly hear from the bathroom or kitchen.

Nora merely smiled and sucked another sweet; he was a good boy to remember the pick-n-mix.

Still, she wasn't dull, Rix delighted in telling his friends, which he had in numbers, as he never really bothered to differentiate between people. Although he did classify them into groups: Friday night pub friends, club friends, dates, past and present. There wasn't any present at the moment. Not since the nice Jean-Phillipe had gone back home, and without a word since.

"Darling, I'm off to meet some friends tonight, but I'll pop-in for eats tomorrow evening," Rix told her as he finished stacking the fridge.

"M & S," Nora chuckled approvingly.

"Lovely," she said, tapping his cheek and stretching up to rub his hair with a broad smile that mirrored her son's. *Nothing like that pig of a father*, she often thought when she looked at her Richy.

"Mind the gel," Rix reproached, stepping out of her reach.

She pulled a face and raised a hand in a pretend slap to his rear as he disappeared out of the door. They loved their games.

"Not the face, not the face," Rix called as he trotted off with a giggle.

Outside on the street, his eyes darted towards the main road. *Nothing much going on*, he thought, as he shrugged his shoulders and carried on walking. It would take him about 20 minutes to get across town, so he decided to give his eyes a chance as he made his way, with no particular pace, to the pub.

He could see Charlotte, Charlie, as he approached the Avenue, throwing her hands about, obviously having some sort of argument or other, but Rix couldn't quite make out who with. He wasn't too sure how he felt about her, something of the night at times, perhaps?

Regardless, he headed off in her direction, eventually his strides stepped into a little run to catch her up.

"Wait up," he called as he got within her earshot.

Charlie turned and made herself smile. It wasn't that she disliked Rix, she quite liked him really, it was just that she thought he got in the way. Officially, of course, if anyone asked, she was sick of so many of the men she knew being gay or married. It made her life easier.

Charlie felt the hands of time ticking; this hadn't been the idea, or any sort of plan, to be 30 and single. And with no prospects on the horizon. But then her career hadn't been her plan either. Parents to thank for that, all right. She understood why that path had been chosen for her, it made sense and kept them all secure. That is what it was all about, she reminded herself with a nod. She was ever alert.

"Hello," she beamed, naturally, her retro styling sitting convincingly on her rounded body and complimenting her manners. Something of another time and place about her.

Rix admired her attention to detail.

"Off to the Arms?" Rix said with a tempting smile, touching her lapel to indicate his approval of her dress and jacket.

She could get away with olive-green, he thought fleetingly.

"Yes. Actually, I'm going to meet Vix."

"That poor love."

Rix grabbed Charlie by the arm and walked with her, in almost marching fashion, speeding up as they got closer to the pub, Charlie keeping in step despite the heels. Their heads were conspiratorially close as they approached. They looked the very picture of a smart young couple, easy and comfortable in each other's company, love on the horizon. Deception was everywhere, it seemed. Despite appearances, they were still trying to 'sus' each other out. They did, after all, both wear a mask to the world.

Vix was already on her second glass of house red when they arrived. She eyed them with a little suspicion at first: *An unlikely alliance*, she thought.

"Have you come to gang up on or sympathise with me," she said with the right degree of sarcasm and a weal smile.

"Lovely," Charlie said, looking at Vix with arched brows.

"Darling girl," Rix said, planting a big kiss on both cheeks and then one other again.

Vix, Rix and Charlie sat and held an inquest into events.

Vix didn't tell them everything; she didn't tell them that she had visited the Arms every day since the screening, with the only reason she could honestly think of being in the hope of seeing Will. She hadn't seen him, but she had seen those men again. The ones she had seen rush the bar, the night they met and she had convinced herself that they were the same ones that had chased Will down the street in Old Portsmouth. She didn't tell them that she had followed them to the railway station and had been petrified when they seemed to have noticed her, even headed towards her, enough to make her scared enough to run. That evening, she had jumped a train and ended up in the suburbs. However, she returned home with what seemed like a plan: she would go to Portsmouth again herself and try to find Will.

"Why?" Charlie demanded, looking a little red in the face as the evening progressed, but losing none of her sharpness as Vix's story unfolded.

"Doesn't seem such a good plan to me either," Rix added, eyeing the young man on his own at the bar. All this talk frightened him, he needed to distract himself and the guy at the bar was an obvious target.

He called over something back in answer to the look, possibly in Polish, before moving further along. Rix just shrugged.

“Look,” Vix realised her tone was getting terse, “I’m really grateful for your advice, both of you, and yes, I am choosing to ignore it all, but.”

“But what?” Charlie slowed her pace too. Vix looked like she was determined.

“I want to find out if this man, Will, is mixed up in drugs or whatever, that I’m OK, not in danger. I also want to know why he has bothered me again, email and setting-up a date he didn’t keep. I’m not standing for it. Not this time.”

Vix was flushed in the face by the time she had finished.

“Well done, girl,” Charlie said empathically.

“Go Vix, go,” Rix concurred, smiling broadly at her before allowing his eyes to dart in all directions. He suddenly felt quite satisfied with himself. He had been noticed.

Chapter 11

The train arrived on time which Vix took as a good omen; that and the fact that every bit of the journey had joined up nicely, without a hitch or blip. She also had someone to meet at the other end.

Between them, both Charlie with her intra-university networking site and Rix with his advertisement in the newspaper, had been great. His wording had needed adjusting, of course, as he had modelled it on the one he had placed for himself during a lean patch. He also made a pitch on a range of social media he played with; those he used in a professional capacity mostly but not exclusively. He meant to crack this one himself.

It had produced results, but Rix didn't divulge any more than that, so alarm bells had started to sound a little in Vix's head. Or should have done if she could have thought about anything other than making this journey and meeting up with this Evie, her one result, who had come forward from the shadows. This result was spot on, unlike a few of the responses they had allocated to dissect between them. It never ceased to amaze her what a shady world existed out there, peopled, by characters, who would say or do anything for some dosh. Vix was glad that she had a woman to meet who claimed to be a friend of Will's, which all appeared to stack up to everyone's agreement. She was determined to be positive, but keep alert. She had promised them that. Both Charlie and Rix were so closely involved with all this now, they spoke of little else.

The harbour station was quite sleepy when Vix arrived; it was like getting off a passenger ferry to go on holiday somewhere she thought, with that air of expectation about it all. She kept pace with the other travellers and loped ahead, slightly unsure on alighting the train. A board walk of sorts lead straight to the barriers, it was slightly inclined and the sea lapped about beneath. The early October sun was soft and welcome, a breeze blew up across the gangway, the chill diminishing slightly the holiday feel of day. She knew she shouldn't feel like that anyway, after all, she was in Portsmouth on serious business. But Vix was excited, if not a little nervous.

On the main street, she checked her text message: "Head out on to the main road, cross over and the pub was there." She stepped ahead, just avoiding a brave prowling cat in her path as it sort to dodge the people who ploughed their way out.

It was an old building, Victorian probably, with etched glass and dark wooden carving around the windows, once grand and now covered in advertising slogans in gaudy orange and clashing pink: Pie-n-pint, Early doors 241 and the like. It looked and certainly felt as if it had fallen on hard times. So did the clientele.

"A coffee please, Americano, black," Vix said, putting down her large bag by the counter.

"A black coffee is it?" asked a thin, balding man in his late 40s; he was probably younger in years but not in experience maybe, and it showed, she nodded and thought about his dead-eyed look as she waited. He stared as he held out his hand for payment for the flat looking dark liquid spilling out onto the saucer from an unbalanced cup.

"Fine, thanks," Vix nodded.

She smiled and disappeared with her drink into a booth by the window. A few others there looked like travellers too, coming to or going from the ferry or the train station, bags, books and other paraphernalia. A small group of ageing men stood by the bar drinking beer, mainly in silence, apart from a few comments which flew up spasmodically from a weasel-like scruffy haired man reading the paper. It seemed to be the football that caused the consternation and momentary distraction from the beer and their lone thoughts.

When Evie arrived, Vix knew it was her even before her mobile pulsated.

Vix waved her over. She had the air of someone once treated as special or beautiful, although she wasn't conventionally so. She was slim, confident enough in her appearance, with a close-fitting blouse tucked into slim jeans and high-heeled shoes that she walked in with ease. But it was all only just the right side of.

Vix stopped herself. She had become very judgemental in recent weeks, she decided. Anyway, what did she expect?

Evie nodded to Vix as she approached the table and slid into the booth on the opposite side.

"Victoria?" she said, a slight lilt to her voice.

Vix noticed her eyes first. They were slightly hooded and the colour of smoke. Her nose had a slight hook in it from one angle and her lips were poised as if ready to speak. As she sat, Evie pushed her fingers up the back of her neck into the fullness of her hair and shook her head, a side fringe of hair much longer than the rest, in dual tones of gold and black, fell over one half of her face. She gave Vix a piercing look with her exposed eye; she meant to get her measure. Or was she nervous too?

"Call me Vix. Thanks for coming. Can I get you something to drink?"

"No, I'm alright. I'd prefer a walk really, than sitting here, when you're done."

Evie nodded towards the see-through brown liquid in the glass cup that Vix had been served for coffee.

"I'm not sure I really want it, actually."

They shuffled free from the booth, Vix's legs sticking to the plastic leather as her skirt crept up, causing her to stall and shuffle some more as the men beside the bar stared. Evie stood there coolly composed and waiting. She had a hauteur about her, made more so by the expression her mouth set into in repose, and her nose was oddly aristocratic to Vix's mind, like a statue perhaps, from another era. Whatever it was, Vix recognised, Evie was in the driving seat here and she just needed to go with it.

As they walked, Evie lit a cigarette and answered briefly some of the questions that Vix threw at her. She had not meant it to sound like interrogation, but she sensed Evie thought it just that, although she remained even tempered about it all.

She seemed to know a lot of people; nodding at the guy outside the Taxi Cab Office, calling out with a sort of wave to some young women on the opposite side of the road, a smile for the guy in a flashy looking sports car who tooted-her as he parked.

"Dave," she said, as if by way of introduction.

Vix smiled uncertainly in his direction before having to run across the road to keep up with Evie's confident strides.

She made her way towards the imposing grey walls that ran parallel with the road. At the grand old entrance gate, that once led to a wharf, a working dock, Evie was stopped and held in conversation by an older looking women with blond hair.

Vix was secretly glad to be able to catch her breath while they talked; she was red-faced after trying to keep up and being forced to play chicken with the traffic as it poured into the brash money-spinner that the old dock had become. Restaurants, clubs, hotel, cinema and shops, you name it. The march of time, in action, progress. Vix stopped herself being cynical.

Evie, of course, gave it no mind.

The older woman eyed Vix as she approached them.

"This is Madge."

Evie touched the woman's arm and gave her a brief smile.

"It'll turn up, lover."

Vix noticed that Madge was quite a bit older than she had first thought; her t-shirt dress with leggings and a denim jacket sat oddly on her when viewed up close. She also noticed that she was wearing a poorly fitting wig.

"Wee, I didn't know that," Madge said in an incredulous tone, as if discovering something almost shocking.

"OK then, cocker."

Evie patted Madge's arm again before she strode off with Vix in tow.

"Friend of yours?"

"No, more than most; I just look out for Madge, it's not been an easy life."

Vix didn't like the hard expression in Evie's eyes when she spoke.

They continued to walk, through into a new world behind the walls; a strikingly tall apartment block with a celebrity chef restaurant below made immediate impact; she wondered to herself why she hadn't noticed it before, the blue of the façade was surely visible for miles. She supposed it was part of her state of mind at the time; first hoping to be 'love-struck' having been whiskered away by Will, then so let down, so deceived and so bloody angry.

The newly paved avenues boasted lushly planted tubs and troughs, elegantly poised alongside the designer boutiques and seating for the café culture they had created. The place exuded affluence, energy and aspiration. There was a brash positivity about the place, from the manmade channel of water that divided the strip to all those people who defied the English weather, imagining themselves abroad or something, as they sipped their cappuccinos and espressos. The yachts at the far end in the real sea added to the illusion, she guessed. Certainly the smell of foreign cigarettes was everywhere, and voices. Lots of money, or access to it. That's what it all said.

Evie appeared oblivious to it all. She seemed to walk through her life in blinkers, focussed on where she was going, or wanted to get.

"You keeping up?" she laughed as they crossed between some shops and apartments, towards what looked like a normal street again. There were some houses before they crossed over and walked through an archway or break in the wall and turned out into the embarkation area of the ferryboats that headed across the channel and to the Isle of Wight. Vix tried to take it in, memorise it if possible. Lorries, coaches, cars, bikes and a few foot passengers, made their way on board and a group of school kids in a mini-bus waved relentlessly to the passing world.

It was noisy, especially as they approached the main road again, snaking around the old dock yard walls, and Vix wasn't exactly sure what Evie was saying to her, so she said nothing back to her for a moment. Evie stopped as they cleared the main road and lit another cigarette by the dip in the wall.

"There are some benches round here in a bit. We'll sit and chat there."

Vix started to try to recall the place as they walked through the old narrow streets, passed a pub, a restaurant now by the look of things, and the fish market. *Yes*, Vix nodded instinctively to herself, she felt knew it.

She looked for the row of old tall houses with steps up to narrow front doors with shiny brass knockers, the wide path across the dock for the fishing vessels, the square solid pub with the painted mural. She remembered all this, it was where she had stayed when she attended the wedding reception. Now she wanted desperately to remember more about Will, now that she was actually back in this place. But Vix found herself thinking about those other lives she had recalled from these very streets with the help of Dai Stanley and she shivered. Will and the dead kept close company.

Vix found herself not running any longer to keep up with Evie, she just felt drawn in the direction of the sea. There was Broad Street, Bath Square. Where were those other lives?

Vix stood and looked out across to the Gunwharf shoreline and the Spinaker Tower, and the Victory beyond, and stilled herself while Evie sat on the bench and relit her cigarette.

"Listen," she said from her seat, "I know we've chatted a fair bit now, about Will and everything, but I think we should talk about the film."

Vix was suddenly shaken from her thoughts and the sounds of a fiddle, laughter and those screams, as she, eyes momentarily locked, stared across the harbour. She made herself cross to the bench; she realised she would have to tell Evie more if she was going to learn more herself in return.

"Yes, it is filming, recording, if you like the findings of the research team working from the university."

"Right. And it said in the advert that you wanted to trace Will as part of this study, is that right? Or something like that, I've got the cut out at home," Evie dragged on her cigarette.

"Yes, I'm really interested in the wedding reception, by the Victory, over there, you said Will went to one on that day and…"

Vix pointed across the water, trying to recall what Rix had put in the ad, as Evie's experienced eyes scrutinised her.

"They are tying up some past lives and modern events, that kind of thing," Vix continued, still not sure what to say or how quickly she could risk blurting out what she really needed to know. She had expected to listen, not explain her motivation. She was thrown.

"Look, I'm OK talking about Will, but I thought there might be a chance to get involved in a film or something. I don't mind if it's historical or whatever, as long as I get paid for it, or some work out of it. I've mentioned it to some of the other girls."

Evie smiled at a couple of very smart older men who walked by with two small dogs, who nodded back to her.

"They're a nice couple," she said before turning back to Vix with a proposition.

"Listen, I've got to get moving in a bit. So, you tell me what's in it, really, for me and I'll let you know if I can help."

"I want to know where Will is," Vix swallowed hard. She'd said it.

"I haven't seen him since the day of the wedding and between you and me," Evie stopped suddenly. "You're not taping me or anything, are you? You're not the old Bill, are you girl?"

Vix straightened on the bench and shock her head fervently.

"Certainly not."

"It's OK, I just ought to be careful, no, you're alright, you're not the type and you've got honest eyes."

She smiled at Vix then, an altogether different smile, but it was only brief and soon over.

"Please, I just want to know, purely personal, but connected to the research project and to this place. And now you, since you got in touch."

"I've known Will for about 10 years. He started me off. He was alright back then. I even thought we were an item once. Times change, things change. I haven't seen him lately, as I said, but that's not unusual, in his line."

So, they were not in a relationship, Vix registered, before reminding herself to listen to Evie.

"The police contacted me during their investigation, they know our connection more than likely and they obviously know what he's up to."

"Which is?"

Vix's question was met with large staring hostile eyes. Vix did not want confrontation. She scrambled her thoughts, she needed to keep the conversation going, she needed more and Evie looked dangerously like clamming up.

"It's OK, don't be alarmed."

"As I was saying, what's in it for me?"

Evie looked her square on, her smokey eyes smouldering now.

Vix took out her purse and handed Evie a £50 note, picked up especially for this purpose.

"I don't know if the research team will come here to film, but I'll put them in touch. In the meantime, I want to know why Will has tried to contact me, since the wedding fiasco and why the police think I might be in danger. Hopefully, this will do on account?"

Vix pushed the note into Evie's hand.

"I haven't told you that much so far, I could tell you other stuff," she said, retrieving the money and slipping it into her jean pocket.

"I've got to go now, I'll be about half-hour, maybe some more, you can never tell at this time of day. Get yourself a drink in there, they do grub too."

Evie pointed to the pub beside the water's edge as she walked off disappearing across Bath Square.

It was a warm and sunny afternoon, Vix's fish and chips had been served wrapped in paper, a house speciality, and the draught cider had gone down well and reminded her of home as she sat there, just looking out to sea, her head full of thoughts as the afternoon drifted on.

Somehow, the Will she had met and this Evie didn't seem to fit.

Some of the ferryboats came in close, like the side of a house suddenly appearing; smaller vessels darted about towards the green painted Marina entrance across the water or back out again through unseen channels into the Solent. Grey battleships sat at a distance beyond a hazy throng of sailing craft, fishing boats and white sporty toys of boats that span as they turned in foamy waters.

A flotsam of people came and went as well, they swept around Vix continuously. They looked over at the modern waterfront or historic ships and laughed, chatted and created a haze of excitement as she simply sat there in contemplation; still more questions than had been answered and the day was petering away.

Evie's text was straight to the point: I'm sending a car over now, look out for one.

Vix didn't stop to think, not any longer, a whole afternoon spent doing that had only produced even more confusion. She did as instructed, waving down the slow-moving vehicle as it approached at a crawl at the bend in the road.

"It's alright love, I know where I'm taking you," the driver pronounced as she got in.

The house he pulled up outside of was old and had faded coloured walls, as did the other houses in the row, a sort of pastel rainbow of lemon-yellow, pea-green and pink with an occasional white redundant shutter open against the wall.

"That one, there love, 18."

He smiled before driving off with: "Evie's sorted the fare," in his broad accent.

Vix knocked despite the door being open.

"Up here," Evie shouted.

The passage way led along to 'B', down to 'A', before a large painted finger signed up for flats 'C' and 'D'.

The carpet was worn and the stairs creaked as Vix followed Evie's voice and the pointing finger upwards.

An awful sweet pungent smell met her and she almost gagged. But little else prepared her for what she saw: every corner of the room, every inch of space, floor and surface, lay deep in debris and filth.

Evie merely stood there, transfixed almost, but not exactly in shock.

Vix zoomed in on clothes discarded randomly across the carpet, interrupted every so often by newspapers and ashtrays, piled high with stumped out cigarette ends.

She quickly raised her hand to her mouth as she saw the scales, the tell-tale white powder and the blade. Little plastic bags lay like confetti across the dusty stained floor.

"Bastard," she heard Evie breath, as if talking to herself.

Her eyes worked the room for something.

Piles of takeaway trays: kebab, fried chicken, pizza. They were all there, they stuck out from under the flimsy table and chair. The bags lay open displaying the noxious contents, spilling out indiscriminately onto any available space, all in varying stages of decay.

Cups, glasses and plastic drinks bottles with pipe holes spilt out the remaining foul contents, projecting out from under the unmade bed. Magazines, empty spirit bottles and the Racing Post lay at a hypothetical arms distance away by the base, the stale air and the odour of the place made Vix really nauseous with a sudden urge to run out. Instead, she turned to Evie.

"What is this all about?" she said quietly.

Evie stood silhouetted against the splashed and stained walls. The small room held all this mayhem together, like the secret that it was. This was not the Will of the outside world. That was for sure.

"This is his gaff," Evie said, "he's got several, though. Keeps moving. He has plants in some. I thought you ought to see it for yourself."

Vix couldn't quite adjust her thoughts quickly enough and just stared unblinkingly at Evie who shook her head at her, turning gum over in her mouth, before turning away to open a drawer.

"I'm taking a risk."

Vix tried to fast-forward to see Will's face; put him in context, see him, and she just could not, not this depravity. It didn't fit.

"Will lived here?"

Vix's voice was almost a whisper.

"Yes, and no, as I said. Look in here."

Evie pushed a narrow door into a tiny bathroom with her foot as she seemed to find what she was looking for in the drawer and slipped it into her bag. Venturing just inside the threshold she pushed the door further and watched as Vix's eyes closed tight shut.

"Filthy sod," Evie shrugged him off with a short laugh as she turned her attention to the window.

Vix forced herself to look again at the scene.

The images swirled before her: the toilet, the basin and the shower all caked in grime, soiled, begging belief that anyone could actually live like this, let alone Will. She gasped for air, but it was putrid. This wasn't right.

More things lay discarded, grouped on the floor, some look abandoned in a hurry in the shower tray. She could only guess at the use of some of the things.

"Look," Evie sighed.

Vix really wanted to escape, but then noticed the red-brown stains on the tiled wall, clinging to the grout, caked and old was her guess. Her head thumped with confusion she felt and very, very angry. He always did that to her. She felt sordid as well seeing this, all over again.

"They're old… That's old blood," Evie mouthed as Vix forced herself to look again.

"You alright up there?" a voice called up.

“On our way down now, lover.”

Evie grabbed Vix by the arm and led her out of the room.

“It’s the car. We’ve gotta get out of here now. Come with me, I’ll drop you back.”

Vix followed silently and remained so as she sat reframing the images she had seen as they drove off down the once pretty seaside road, now made hideous to her. Not to mention the lives he must have ruined.

“Will isn’t the man you thought he was, I’ll be bound,” Evie said lighting a cigarette, oblivious, as the driver was, to the stuck on ‘No Smoking’ notice.

“But I have to admit, it was OTT, even for him.”

“Do you think that he’s in danger, I mean, real danger? Do you think something has happened to Will?”

Evie looked at Vix with a mixture of sympathy and disbelief.

‘What I don’t get is why the likes of you would go anywhere near his sort,” Evie mouthed through the smoke, before turning her head away.

“Look, there was an interesting coincidence that I wanted to pursue involving him, I’ve tried to explain,” Vix was pale now, washed out and Evie could see it.

“You best go back home, as soon as, I’ll let you know if I hear anything. You keep me posted on that filming lark, too.”

She didn’t need to talk to the driver, but they certainly communicated as he swerved in to drop her off.

Evie waved very briefly and was gone. Vix was on her own.

***

The sound of heavy shoes on the cobbles, so close, troubled her. When she turned, they seemed to disappear. Voices drifted out and up from the houses, passed through the alleys and gathered at the water’s edge. But Vix saw no one.

Her room was small, the window closed, yet still the echoes, still the sounds.

She realised she knew them. She knew the names that they were calling, their words and accents, their story.

Vix climbed out of bed and went to the window but was afraid; she wanted to open the curtains, open the window and speak.

How do you speak to those from that other world? But at that moment they didn't seem so distant in time at all. They were there, now, laughing and crying; the girl by the quayside stood and wept while the children played. The party throbbed with vitality and hope. The bride screamed. The gang came. Will ran to Vix that night, and what she saw all was so real.

Chapter 12

"Charlie, I need your help."

Vix sat back and re-read her mail and wondered why he only communicated in this way to her.

She also wondered why Charlie had been less than sympathetic when she had asked her to meet Will for her. Well, not exactly meet him, but go to the 'Arms' and keep a look out until she had chance to get there herself. Vix's instructions were simple: text her about every man that came in who might be Will.

Charlie was getting fed up with it all, it was almost an obsession; although she would probably present as being annoyed at being free and available herself as Vix would accept that. Charlie was aware that she needed to monitor the situation but she didn't have to enjoy the role. After all, she wasn't meant to be continuously at work, surely, not even they could expect that. She wondered if that was what life had been like for her conscientious committed parents, in fact still was, in their line of work you simply didn't just retire.

However she viewed it, Charlie still couldn't understand why Vix would want to meet the guy who had been nothing but a pain since her first encounter with him. Especially now she knew that he lived like a degenerate. Christ, Vix had even chosen to disbelieve that what she had seen with her own eyes had anything to do with 'her' Will. She wasn't sure about Evie either. In fact, Charlie pondered if Vix had even told the woman everything. She had definitely clammed up about it. Charlie needed to find out more about her.

"OMG. Come now," Charlie texted Vix as quickly as she could.

Him? Tonight he was wearing his new tweed jacket. Someone should tell him just what a prat he looks at times, Charlie thought fleetingly. She then felt quite angry inside, a sudden rush of emotion which she controlled with her usual flare. Whatever Vix wanted or expected Charlie wasn't exactly sure, but she knew it wasn't this.

Dai Stanley looked pleased with himself as he walked in adjusting his collar, eager little eyes dancing around the bar, broad smile hovering, waiting to develop at the right time for the right person.

Dai spotted her immediately. Charlie thought for a moment he looked annoyed; certainly the smile didn't erupt across his red face as might have been expected.

"Hello, there," he said, with forced jollity, as he raised his free hand to her.

Charlie noticed that he was carrying something in a carrier bag.

"Waiting for someone?" he asked as he approached. "I don't want to intrude."

"Sit down."

Charlie slid across the bench seat, but made sure that she kept her eye on the main entrance.

"I'll get us a drink."

"No, allow me," Dai insisted, straightening up and walking to the bar with sudden interest.

"Shall I get one in for your friend?" he called back to Charlie, "It's red for Victoria, isn't it?"

"Yes," Charlie answered him, but it troubled her. Why should he automatically assume it would be Victoria? He also had a rather smug attitude about him tonight which irritated her more than usual.

"There you are."

"Cheers."

"Oh look, there's your little friend Victoria coming now."

This time Charlie considered smacking him; after all, he was behaving like a bumptious school boy, and at his age. Charlie was not sure what to expect from Vix either, after her trip in pursuit of lover-man, Will. Both of her companions might be too much to for her this evening. But here, she had to be.

Charlie softened, however, as Vix approached, looking pale and a little agitated.

"I've got you a nice large glass of house red," Dai proclaimed, pushing the glass towards Vix with his brightest smile.

Charlie cringed.

"And I have some very interesting news for you."

"Get on with it then, man," Charlie glared to emphasise her irritation, but her words appeared lost on him.

"Yes Dr Stanley, please go on,"

Charlie recognised that note of defeat in Vix's voice as she gave her demonstration of polite attention to the unwanted man.

"Dai, please," he said, touching Vix's hand.

"Well?" Charlie demanded, eyeing him for an uncomfortably long while.

"One of my chaps went digging about a bit, after seeing the film of your regression. And guess what?"

The two women both stared back at him, nodding encouragement and trying to look composed.

"They found 'your' wedding," he announced, before taking a long slurp of his ale.

"The wedding in Portsmouth at the time of the Napoleonic wars, when the press gang interrupted the celebrations themselves, by taking men for the navy, for Nelson's fleet destined for Trafalgar."

Vix sat back. She could say nothing, just listen as Dai Stanley continued on in his blinkered way, furnishing the details that the research team had uncovered; it definitely uncovered a perfect match of accounts to what Vix had experienced under hypnosis.

"It is compelling evidence, Victoria," he finished, venturing his hand towards hers once again.

Charlie could read Vix's expression, demeanour and body language usually, but despite searching for clues, this seemed different, she couldn't quite fathom what was going on with her. She looked at her quizzically, nothing gave.

"Are you OK, Vix?" they both asked her almost at once. She was underwhelmed and it was strange.

"I'm fine. Thank you, Dai, for sharing that, it was really very interesting."

Dai looked as if her almost dismissive response had physically hurt him as he fell back into his seat.

"The thing is, I'm here to meet someone and I think I would rather come and look at the evidence myself, if that's OK, at another time. All this has been an unsettling experience for me you see."

Dai seemed to both like and then not like Vix's response, as he lurched forward from the padded settle, his smile dissipated into the air. Charlie supposed he had wanted to spend the evening boring them, well, Vix; talking himself up, the worldly-wise professor imparting his knowledge to the poor grateful young thing. Charlie reminded herself sharply that she worked for him and needed to stop being quite so vitriolic.

She also wanted to hear how Vix really had got on in Portsmouth and to try to catch a glimpse of this Will character, if he turned up this time, just to confirm it was him. He had been in contact again, so why not? It was another email, though, coward.

"Might as well have another drink while you wait for the mystery man," Dai pronounced, getting his smile back.

The women said nothing, just watched him go, watched the door and looked out through the windows.

"Maybe he came before and I missed him. I mean, I don't know really what he looks like, do I?"

"I've bored you with it enough," Vix regained herself.

"Apart from the tall, handsome, confidant hair and deep dark eyes, you mean?"

They both laughed at that as Charlie continued to embellish the description of him, adding a series of previously undisclosed deformities that her friend could have been keeping from her. It was childish but broke the frosty atmosphere.

"I can assure you he is all in one piece, isn't ginger or fat."

They both nodded and smiled as Dai Stanley approached. *She's back*, thought Charlie.

"And English, I presume?" Charlie asked as they accepted their drinks.

"Now, where were we?" he said, sipping his real ale.

Chapter 13

Mr Heskey closed the door with determination; he was going to do it. He stumbled down the concrete path, sticks loosely in hand, bag on his shoulder, and considered how many days he could summon up the courage to use the thing. He had been attracted to the claret wine colour and the sturdy black foot rests; Sheila said that the basket would come in handy for the shopping too. He was the man of the house, the only one of the house now and he needed the challenge. It kept him going.

It was one of those days when the breeze has more of a lasting chill than the sun and blue of the sky suggested; autumn was kicking in. Best make the most of it.

With that, Mr Heskey positioned himself with precision and pulled himself comfortably into the seat of his mobility scooter, tucked his sticks into the slot he reserved at the back and headed off.

He was not a pavement man. He didn't want people jumping out of his way as if he were an invalid or a baby in a pram. No, for Mr Heskey this was no different to the real scooter he had owned briefly in his youth. He told himself that often.

He turned out of the drive and made his way to the high road, just beating a smart blue car. The low sun dazzled him briefly but he took the plunge and turned right with a forceful wave of his hand. They would see him. They could stop faster than he could.

He was set then, straight on, left at the lights, red ahead, they would turn nicely green by the time he got to them, then left again and along by the shore today. That would lift him. Perhaps, this wasn't such a bad contraption after all. Mrs Hodges had called it a 'death trap'. Silly woman.

He noticed that the tide was out, the thick green-grey mud was moist and shiny; he briefly thought of the old days and larking about in the creek. Him and Frankie digging for lug worm and pulling out that little old rowing boat belonging to his uncle Alf. Never caught much. *Happy days*, he thought to himself as he slowed slightly to a crawl along the familiar route, Portchester Castle still strong and silent in the background, the smell of earth and sea, the gulls still a bloody nuisance.

Why not stop?

Mr Heskey wasn't really impetuous, not anymore, but today seemed different. With a quick directional wave he pulled over, sharply left into the lay-by by the fish-n-chip shop. That would do it. She turned well, he considered as he stopped the engine and sat there breathing deeply, looking at the view and assuring himself that the air would do him good.

"Morning," a young woman with a toddler nodded to him as they passed.

Apart from that no one was about, just the streams of passing traffic, the squawk of gulls and a light breeze that cooled Mr Heskey as he clambered off his scooter and made his way slowly towards the shoreline.

He smiled, he'd have something to tell Sheila about now, if she called.

The water was visibly moving around the old castle and he could see a boat or two in the distance, but it only surged slightly and spasmodically, sucked in near the wormholes. Where he stood, spits of water limply trickled down the grooves in the mud that had formed, reminiscent of a murky desert landscape across the creek. That familiar smell, now tinged with petrol and rotten debris: the discarded cans, bottles and polystyrene takeaway containers. Mr Heskey shook his head and continued his slow passage along. He thought that he heard voices but no one was there when he turned around. But he noticed some movement, some bubbling up almost, towards a little bank that had formed, an island sticking proud from the rivulets that passed either side of it.

Soon, the sea would return. It would look better then. But he had a fondness for the mud.

There was someone there. He heard the scream, sharp and piercing, a woman's scream. It carried closer, then he saw her, she ran his way, shaking her head, a dog close at her heels suddenly.

"Someone's in the creek, in the mud, get help. No mobile," she almost cried as she spoke.

Mr Heskey stood suddenly very still. But, before he realised he had pushed his sticks into the soft wet earth and propelled himself across to where the women had pointed. The stick sunk in, but he kept going. The breeze kept coming, but he felt hot, his hands swollen and locked around his stick, he kept moving forward.

He saw a hand. Yes, it was a large hand and it reached up to him out of the mud, mottled black and green and swollen. He had to help.

"Hold on," he heard himself saying.

As he got as near as he could, he lowered himself onto one knee, then the other, using his stick for support. He looked about him, he was alone; he couldn't see or hear the woman, just the distant throb of an engine.

Mr Heskey reached out, kept reaching, his fingers touched the poor persons outstretched hand and he pulled with everything he could muster.

He dug in his stick for leverage, he pulled back his entire body in his search for a bit more strength to help save the poor soul.

The mud spluttered and a shoot of water sprung out and up; the glutinous mess moved and the hand moved.

Mr Heskey let out a loud shout, half laughing, half crying as the pain in his chest grew greater and he fell backwards onto the soft, wet mud around him. The hand came with him. Just a single hand. Mr Heskey lay on the ground with the dead detached hand firmly in his grasp and heard himself scream.

At a little distance, a man leaned out of his large blue car and nodded, as if to his own satisfaction.

"Job done," he said, before driving off.

Chapter 14

"Yes. And yes again!

Yes, but I need to go now, Mother.

What?

Of course, see you about six. Bye-bye.

Oh, Vix just walked in.

Yes, sends her love.

Yes, will do, darling."

Rix smiled at Vix whilst she slid quietly through into his office, the aroma of coffee and his favoured cinnamon topping catching her nostrils as she waved towards the phone and Rix's mother. It felt comfortable, she decided, being around Rix. It felt familiar, like she had known him years. And that was good.

She had met his mother for tea, a request to keep her happy; something to tell her friends about if they made any of those silly remarks about her Rich. If he wanted to settle down with a girl he would, whatever anyone thought.

"Unusual, but great company," she had told Charlie about Rix's mother, her raised eyebrows being the only response expected Vix had said no more. But she liked her and envied Rix and his mother, their warm relationship. It was certainly very different from hers with her parents. But not different from what she expected, particularly after what had happened, although she wouldn't allow herself to dwell on her marriage right now.

"I hope you don't mind, I'm looking at this regression stuff again."

Rix swivelled the monitor round to show her what he was looking at with a slightly apprehensive smile.

He had noted her appearance of late and she hadn't looked herself somehow. She looked thin rather than slim and pale, even for her. It aged her a little as well he thought, but he wouldn't say that. She had never been exactly bubbly but she seemed almost withdrawn by comparison these days too.

Rix decided to be careful about her, gentle, and smiled as he pulled up a chair which he patted invitingly for her to sit on, next to him.

He guessed that Vix found it hard to connect to that person on the screen, in repose on a couch, sounding so different, talking about such strange non-sense from a past she was adamant she knew nothing of, yet she was there, looking just like her ordinary self, no mistaking who it was. A thin pale version of herself with flamed cheeks and blank eyes, but nonetheless, Vix. He could only imagine its impact, he knew that he couldn't have handled it as well, in the circumstances. He shivered slightly, but fascination drove him on. Perhaps, that was the way of it for her too. Rix enjoyed his new knowledge and meant to know even more, nothing would stop him delving further. He was entering new realms of discovery.

"Go ahead. Might keep you company for a bit if that's OK?"

"Of course," he turned to her briefly to smile. "Waiting for Charlie?" he asked, his eyes now fully captured by the image on his screen.

Vix automatically nodded and smiled briefly before she too turned her attention to the screen – it had to be done.

"I was a Top Man. Not many got higher than me as often without a fall or two. Not many lived if they did, to say so. It paid me well, but not as well as war and bounty did, but more than the powder-monkey I started as. I made my money by daring and doing what an honest man shouldn't aspire to; on one trip alone, I took more than a year's wage, just one voyage and you could be free. Some spent it as fast as they had made it. Some left the service and set themselves up, offering all manner of services in the dockside alleys. The wise took what they could back to their former lives, to their farms or homes if they had one. Some like me, kept going back for more, what else had I known? Children made up a fair part of the navy, after all. And then there are those, if truth be told, that would be destined for the prison hulks lying nearby. And the free-slaves. Their choice was made for them. And for those maimed and weak. There were all manner of men, of all nations and dispositions, and strong stubborn women too. I was friend to all and none. I still live amongst strangers, but we have a fraternity: we ask no questions and look to our own."

***

Rix saw the tears rolling down her cheeks as Vix sat silent and still next to him.

"He's dead," she said eventually. "I had a text from Evie you know, his friend," she continued quietly.

"What did she say?" Rix turned off the machine, shuddering at his insensitivity despite his earlier promise to himself. He turned to face her, grabbing her hands in his so that she would face him too.

"Just that: Will is dead. Nothing any more than that. So final."

She trailed off, her head drooping slightly, her eyes downcast, away from Rix's gaze.

"I'll know more from Charlie really."

She recovered herself and gave Rix an appreciative smile as she explained,

"Charlie was trawling the newspapers online and found the article about Will, found dead and…"

"Yes?" he prompted, his curiosity getting the better of him again.

"He wasn't all in one piece. They had cut off his hand. Stealing their 'stuff'. I guess; I don't know really. Charlie's bringing a copy of it over for me to see."

"Do you want me to get online…?"

As Rix said it, the horror in her eyes made him instantly remorseful again.

"I'm so sorry, love. So bloody insensitive, that's me."

Rix piqued, jumping to his feet and prowling the room, holding his head in his hands. It was dramatic, but that was him, Vix knew it to be as sincere as he felt at that moment.

"No, you're alright. I should have done it for myself anyway, not ask Charlie. I couldn't face it. Thanks for trying to help," she said, standing to place a thoughtful hand upon his arm, with the best smile that she could muster.

They both turned as Charlie entered. Whatever she felt, she didn't show it. She smiled politely at Rix and walked straight to Vix with an A4 envelope.

"It's all in here," she said straightforwardly as she stepped back to lean against the office wall with a large sigh.

Vix pulled the envelope to her for a moment before reaching for the opening. She pawed tentatively through the neatly compiled collection of articles, laying them out methodically on the desk as she read them. They were all dated and in order: first, the missing Will, then the appeals for information, the investigations, the human-interest angle, then the body. Then, identification. All there to see. Unbelievably coherent.

"I'll get more coffee," Rix announced, leaving quickly with his tobacco pouch.

Charlie inspected the various prints, memos and cartoons that lined the walls of the office before settling on the padded chair nearest the window.

'When they have you by the balls, your heart and mind does follow', pinned up high, and large enough for all to see.

Charlie noticed Rix smoking and talking by the front steps of the building and smiled slightly to herself as she scanned the street below.

Probably having a gossip, she thought as she turned her attention back into the room, perhaps with just a little envy of his carefree ways.

Vix's expression kept changing as she read, her eyes scanned the information she had been presented with for hidden clues about Will and his life; she looked perplexed, alarmed and could not disguise her upset. She bit her lip as she turned over the sheets of copied paper.

Charlie sat patiently but detected a change in her demeanour. Vix pulled her chair in closer to the desk, picked up a sheet with a picture squeezed into the body of the text, holding it quite close, then throwing it down and smiling, or was it practically laughing.

Charlie forced herself forward, not knowing exactly how to react, wanting to make sure that Vix was actually smiling and yes, audibly laughing as she stared at the newspaper article. She needed to know how to respond.

Rix returned and pushed his way in. His eyes swiftly moved from Vix to Charlie in askance. They were both moved and worried by her response. Laughter wasn't what they expected.

"It's not him."

Rix put the coffees down with a thump as he tore over to see what Vix was looking at.

"What on earth do you mean?" Charlie erupted. "His woman has told you that he is dead and the papers are confirming all the details. You can't just say that it isn't him. Please Vix, you're just, well, just in denial."

"Leave it, leave it now, let's have a look, very calmly."

Charlie arced her brows at Rix's new statesmanlike stance.

"Look," Vix said firmly, getting both their attention.

"There is a description: first, distinct tattoo on his neck, of a bird. Never saw that. Then, yes, here it states that he had a scar running the length of his jaw. Never saw that either. He was said to be 5' 8". My Will was well over 6'."

They both looked at her then, but said nothing.

Vix stood and held the picture of the dead man to the light of the window for them to see.

"This Will is also bald, has a darker complexion and look here, 'the missing man has unusual coloured eyes, with one being blue and the other green'. That is what it says," Vix ended with a look that defied challenge.

"Well, it sounds very different from the one you described to me," Rix said.

"And you saw him, on the night I met him,"

"Well, couldn't swear to that, it was a bit messy that night, wasn't it?"

Rix moved to open the tops off the carry-out coffees.

"Well, Charlie?" Vix asked, needing her reasoning, which she trusted, even if it wasn't the same as her own.

"Vix, you are right, this isn't the man you met. It also isn't the man that you have been going off to Portsmouth to find out about either, is it? This Evie woman has been feeding you information about someone else. A not very nice someone else as well. Drug dealer, pimp?"

"And he stole from his own," Rix interjected, blowing on his coffee.

"Yes, I realise that."

"Do you also realise that they don't know that? That they think you are linked to him in some way, perhaps in a way that involves their money or whatever?" Charlie pulled in her bottom lip as if to keep herself from saying more.

Vix swallowed hard and looked from friend to friend. She had only concerned herself with finding her Will, of establishing that it wasn't her Will that was found dead and mutilated. It drove her. She needed to do it.

"You could be in danger."

Both women turned on Rix as he spoke. Charlie chastised him, but Vix's look registered that she understood. It wasn't the first time she had been made aware of the danger. She needed to get real and she needed to get to that place herself.

"While we're on the subject, men, well some men," Charlie looked at Rix and nodded as she spoke. "I have another disclosure for us. Those emails."

"Yes," Vix suddenly became alert. "Certainly this guy was dead when I was still getting emails to meet up."

A small smile began to form on Vix's face as she spoke and her enlarged eyes fixed on Charlie desperately.

"I'm sorry to tell you Vix, but 'your' Will didn't send those emails to you. It was in fact Dai Stanley, and believe me, I've had serious words with him about it as well."

There was a shocked silence, Rix put down his coffee and held his hand across his mouth. Vix looked crest fallen. Charlie's anger resonated as she continued to explain what she had uncovered about Dai Stanley, sparing nothing despite the horror on her friend's face.

"Don't have any more to do with him and all this transgression stuff," Rix announced, escorting Vix with a gentle arm about her shoulder to a chair and placing a coffee securely in her two hands.

"But I feel so drawn to the place, to those people I describe, they are so real. Why does life have to be so complicated?" Vix said through emerging tears.

"Look, you're not in the best frame of mind at the moment. You need to rest and get this Will out of your system," he said rubbing her arm.

"And be careful," Charlie said before claiming the last coffee and turning to stand by the window.

She looked back at Vix immediately as if to speak but didn't. She just stood and stared as she drank, picking up her mobile to text.

“How much do you know about V’s past? C.” Rix looked across to Charlie, who continued to sip her coffee and stare at the scene below whilst she waited for him to text back.

She might need to enlist his help further.

Chapter 15

The nights were starting to get darker sooner; the openness of people's attitude, their slower pace, relaxed persona, all passed with the summer. October had arrived and so had maybe that slow withdrawal into isolationism which happened for some people, particularly in cities, even the friendlier ones.

Those were his thoughts as he stood in the bus shelter slowly smoking a cigarette, untroubled by anyone. Students newly arrived in the area shuffled along, some self-consciously in their new habitat, on the lookout for comrades or where to hang, clutching the tool of their trade, mobiles with all the apps you would ever need. Some forming groups, over eager to fit in.

The professionals, office workers or whatever started the journey home to their period dwellings on the hill, comfortable places around the green or all the new buildings by the water. The shops were shutting, the traffic increasing, the city was on the move.

He decided to wait just a little longer before crossing over to the entrance. He knew her schedule. He pulled up his hood, threw his cigarette to the ground and jogged over the road with meaning.

"Cheers mate, nice one," he said, grabbing the door from closing as the work weary tenant entered the apartment building. "Always tell myself that the exercise is good for me."

He laughed as the man who let him through nodded his understanding lethargically and with little interest.

"Plonker," he breathed to himself. "That is the right word for him, I'm thinking."

He would climb the stairs, only one flight up, rather than take the lift. He didn't want to talk to anyone else. He stood for a while and watched the lift go up with the pale portly man in it.

Good, he thought, *second floor*.

With that, he quietly opened the heavy safety door and mounted the stairs.

The automatic light went on, he could hear a radio coming from the flat on the half-landing as he passed and the smell of food filtering through passageways as he reached the first floor.

He had to make sure that she wasn't in. There were two flats with front doors near to each other on this floor. Both had brown painted doors, brass numbers and letterboxes. Both had spy-holes.

He pressed himself up close to number 9; pulling out a crumpled envelope, he cupped into his hand together with the small box of chocolates; flowers might have been better, but impractical on this occasion.

He smiled broadly in the direction of the spy-hole and knocked on the door.

No one answered. He waited just a while and then turned to approach number 10.

"Peace offering?" The passer-by quizzed with a shake of his head.

He wasn't sure what to say to the neighbour, so he smiled and nodded his head, shrugged his shoulders and laughed lightly with the man.

"You'll have a long wait now; a bit more suffering, eh?"

He went on his way up the stairs, heavy footed and humming a tune of sorts, until all went quiet as he arrived at his home.

The décor of the block was dated, probably quite smart in its day, but he wondered about the inhabitants now. He had been keeping a keen eye on the place for a while and he was sure that he hadn't seen that man in a week or two. Then he nodded to himself, recalling he had been carrying a suitcase.

"Should have got the lift."

He shrugged and pulled a face to the empty landing.

The old woman lived opposite; she was in her 70s he thought, very smart when she went out, with a little dog. He would hear it if she was in, she always seemed to have it with her. She played bridge on Wednesday afternoon and had a hairdresser visit on Friday mornings, the help came on Monday and Thursday. He liked the order of her life. It was useful to him when people lived like that.

He listened and moved back to number 9.

"Might as well try a knock," he told himself.

Same old routine: body pressed close, chocolates and note in hand, smile on the face, foot at the ready.

No reply.

He bent down and looked through the letterbox. He stood up to check his orientation, to double check it was the correct flat, although he knew that he was right really. It was all planned.

"Get on with it," he told himself sternly.

He returned his attention to the door. He forced his arm through the letterbox as far as it could go and splayed his fingers in the faint hope that a key might be attached to a string or something. No such luck. Not here, not in this bloody country, he mused, disgruntled, as he thought about things.

He took out a credit-sized card with a sharp toughened strip and pushed it through, along by the edge of the door, beside the key hole. It was an old Yale. He heard nothing and nothing moved either. He pulled the door towards him, his hand gripped tightly around the door through the opening. He pulled it to him then kicked it away. Nothing. He was about to resort to brute force and a throbbing shoulder when his foot slipped on the little mat at the entrance declaring 'Welcome'. He jerked forward, banging his head on the number plate, throwing him backwards with a jolt to his neck. And there it was. Hanging in the flowerpot, carefully placed within the ornamental silver-green leaves of the display, the key, with a green string attached to it, just waiting to be pulled out.

He allowed himself a smile before he wondered who it might have been left for. He proceeded anyway and opened the door, closing it behind him deftly.

There was a door either side of the small passageway as he entered. On the left the small bedroom door was open.

"Books, books, boxes and clothes. No comfort for the guest," he said to himself.

Opposite was the bathroom, it had an old looking enamel nameplate: 'Sal de Bain'. He shrugged and raised an eyebrow.

In front of him at the end of the narrow hall was the door to the main room, it was ajar and the last of the days light filtered in, casting flickering shadows in the hall. He heard nothing, so proceeded further.

The floor squeaked as he trod across the boards to put his head into the main room.

"Slowly, slowly," he counselled

Untidy. She probably will not even notice that I have been, flickered through his mind.

He crossed the room, then starting with the shelves, the drawers below them and the window ledges, searched. Brightly patterned cardboard boxes sat along the wall on the floor beneath the window, the lids pressed down in an attempt to push in the contents; some were more successful than others. The spotted box had split at the sides. Only paperwork from what he could see.

He progressed around the room slowly. He was methodical, he didn't want to return, that was always more dangerous. He needed to find what he had been sent for, more perhaps, if something interested him or if he thought it would interest them, more to the point. More interest, more work, more money. He would get enough together to go home. Eventually. Then, he would finish with all this, no more for him, he was determined to live quietly.

The sofa was too large for the room and he bumped into it as he rose up from his ground level search. He stilled himself as a side lamp thudded to the floor, knocked by the arm of the sofa from the little table it had stood on. Nothing. Not one sound. No one heard, or bothered.

"People," he sighed to himself.

The back of the sofa was clear. He had one final wall to check and then turn his attention to the mess in the middle. The coffee table was long and piled at one end with booklets, like a student has; CDs were spread around across the surface, between the remote control, mugs and the hurriedly emptied contents of a bag.

In a hurry this morning, he thought.

There it was. A little silver digital camera. That was what they had asked for.

He picked it up as if it was a precious find at an archaeological dig and placed it securely in his jacket pocket, being careful to zip the contents tightly in.

The front door vibrated slightly as the lift stopped and its door opened with a final bang and judder. He paused. He heard a woman's voice. Then another, a dog barked, he heard keys being jangled. The phone sounded. He could hear the woman's voice, the same woman's voice, asking that you leave her a message as she couldn't come to the phone right now. He swallowed involuntarily and started to perspire. He shocked himself.

"It's Charlie, call me," suddenly jumped out from the answer phone.

"Shit," he mouthed.

He closed his eyes as he looked about him. The window. Only one story up. He swallowed again and moved across. Then he saw her and realised that the voices had gone. He saw the old lady with the dog as well, they were walking together, she was giving the young one something, money, and pointing.

He smiled and breathed deeply before moving swiftly to the front door. He composed himself, opened it confidently, just in case someone was passing, and returned the key to its nest.

"Evening," a man nodded as he passed.

Without hesitation he replied in the same manner and made his way jogging down the stairs and out through the main entrance.

"Come here, Sadie," the woman called to her dog, trying to rein in the retractable lead as it twisted around the young man's feet.

"No problems," he stated, skipping out of the tangle and continuing with his run.

"Here you are," Vix said as she approached with the evening paper she had asked her to buy. "New neighbour?" she asked with a quick smile.

"I don't know, love. They all seem the same to me these days. I thought he was that young man you've been having around lately," she said it with a chuckle.

"But thanks for doing that, it saved me having to go up there, you know I don't like walking that far down when it starts getting dark."

"Of course, a pleasure; I only wish I did know the man, nothing to do with me, I'm afraid."

Vix smiled broadly as they went into the block together.

"Of course, dear, whatever you say."

As he ran off down the road he felt his pocket, *Still safe*, he thought. When he touched the left-hand pocket, it felt oddly flat. Then it dawned on him – he'd left his box of chocolates.

Vix peered at the front room window as she entered with her bag. It was open. She never opened her front window. She quickly pulled it closed, tight, and looked down at the street, empty apart from a feral cat and a jogger who stopped and looked up at her.

She couldn't explain the window, but she didn't notice anything else as she looked around. Nothing else seemed odd as she walked around the rest of the flat, either.

Just that expression on the joggers face puzzled her a bit. As Mrs J would have said they all look the same, it was a generic look these days alright; she wouldn't have recognised him even if she met him, not in all that gear. Could have been a friend of number 6, or some guy from work. Vix smiled at the nonsense running through her thoughts.

She had better things to think about, well, certainly different things to think about.

She noticed her phone flash.

Charlie, she thought. "What now, wait up," she said as she reached over.

As Charlie didn't respond, Vix decided that the mess in front of her had to be dealt with when that up close to it all, it could no longer be ignored. It had claimed pride of place far too long and she made a start, tried at least, to chuck some stuff out and put bits together in some sort of order. Not that she felt like unpacking her boxes much, she didn't think that she would be able to stay in all likelihood. She liked her job well enough, even if it didn't exactly stretch her. They might have termed her over qualified, but she didn't really know anymore what she was actually qualified for. Her future had seemed so clearly defined and mapped out at one time. Then she had met Ash, made plans to travel and do something fulfilling in Africa or the Middle East, or where ever their combined skills and knowledge could take them. It felt brave, sounded glamorous, proved elusive. She had saved hard, took on extra, so had he, of course, the money mounted up but wasn't quite enough. They sold the flat as they wouldn't need it. Vix had meant to return the deposit money her parents had provided. But she could not. Ash had it before she even knew. Vanished.

"I didn't go to work, and your mother go without, so we could fund terrorism!" her dad had exploded.

The thought of it made her feel wretched.

Vix hurried to the kitchen area and found a glass to pour the remains of some wine she had left in the fridge.

"There's nowhere to bloody put anything in here," she said loudly to the air, needing to vent her anger before marching some books into the hallway. She screwed up her eyes, she hadn't remembered the box of chocolates on the hall shelf.

Chapter 16

You could get used to the life. The ship was your mother and father; it fed you and provided for you and kept you in line. To some, it was the only parent they had ever known. But our Will wasn't like that. He'd had a life on the farm until the dockside offered more prospects, more work and money. He was an ordinary man. A handsome youth with manners and some charm. He would always sweet-talk the girls and their mothers too. His learning was not of great significance, but he held a tune and could sing, courtesy of his landlord who had a fancy for it on occasion; 'tis he who had some of the locals schooled in it.

Being of the country, Will was well used to celebrating as only those folks who toil with their hands can, the starting of a season or the bringing of a harvest. Cider time was his favourite, and that was surely the truth as I have witnessed. The songs that they sang then had a different tune; the fiddle was livelier, the beat faster and words were added or taken away according to the company, I would suppose.

Will was well liked and had done well to get the girl, Lotte, to be his wife. Her family were steady people. He had been young when he'd arrived in Portsmouth, but fate had looked favourably upon him and he prospered, like the families of cats that lived by the dockside in harmony, keeping down the rats.

Would he be able to survive the ways of the ship and all which occurred in that life? It was a different world. No kindness, no soft-skinned girl there.

Will's 'best man', Joseph, was not so ordinary; his story was not so comfortable either. He was worldly wise. He had had the benefit of a proper good education, reading, writing, knew the Bible from cover to cover, it seemed to me. He was from the West Indies, a large island called Jamaica, and he told of his mother being born a slave, his father a white gentleman, owner of a plantation. It was he that had provided for his offspring with an education, and a place in the navy.

Some of Joseph's fellows, those plantation men with the twang in their speech, said they only felt safe on board His Majesty's ship, in case they were taken to be slaves once again.

But not so Joseph, he was free and proud, with a local girl for wife, although he still called his ship more home than his rooms in Portsmouth. He had made a good place for himself there, and money too.

Will treasured him for his stories, experiences and ideas. He was strong as well as learned and commanded respect amongst the men. He was a handy man for an officer to know when at sea for a stretch. And that could be a long one and all manner of men needed controlling; especially if rations were short and payment was a long way off and not guaranteed.

We all hardly dared think if Will would survive being taken by the gang and put in such a place on his wedding day.

***

"Charlie, I really don't care. My Will is still alive. I've been approached by someone else about him, and it's not Dai Stanley sending me fake emails this time. Something else odd has happened too. Later V."

As soon as Vix had sent the email she felt rotten, it was too abrupt and out of character. Charlie had been good to her, helpful and kind but she couldn't let her control her. She was grateful that Charlie had kicked Dai into touch for trying to pretend that he was Will in his infantile attempt to get to 'know her better'. But that said, the regression she had agreed to herself, without being unduly pushed into it, and it had been her that had wanted to know more. It was her that had kept asking to see the tapes, understand more about that strange past life she somehow knew so much of. Maybe even taken comfort in.

It was she, after all, that had gone off to Portsmouth and met Evie.

Vix needed to take full responsibility; to do what she thought was right. Not what Charlie wanted her to do. They were not in school anymore.

Vix re-read the response she had just received from a guy calling himself Stefan.

She had nearly binned it, with the other crank mail which her request for information on Will had produced. She didn't realise there were quite so many cranks, or possibly just lonely hearts, out there. She blinked the thoughts away, there was no dwelling on all that right now.

It had all seemed so harmless until she had met Evie and had a glimpse into yet another 'other world', although this time one firmly rooted in the here and now at least.

Will, the gangland drug dealer come pimp, hadn't turned out to be 'her' Will, thank God, but he still had existed, he still had done all those things she had read about, and he had died horribly. They had identified him by the tattoo finally, although why putting together a severed arm with a body without one had taken so long, Vix wasn't quite sure; it might have taken an age for the arm to be washed up, she supposed. She harboured some prejudice against the police after all, and really didn't want to think about that all over again. Of her three Wills, that one was of least interest, although she felt she knew him better after meeting Evie, not to mention all that stuff Charlie had found for her to read. She thought about Evie; now Vix knew he had got her hooked at an early age and then forced her to work for him. She'd done well to stay around; according to the papers a lot in her position ended up in prison, died, disappeared without even being noticed.

Vix thought of the young woman's smoky eyes and edgy manner, and then her smiles for those people on the street. A surrogate family? Like the story of those on the ship in her regression tape, kept reoccurring.

She had stopped contacting Evie now, Will's story was out. He'd ended up giving her a legacy of sorts; some had paid well for her story, before she was given a new identity according to Charlie, who seemed to know rather a lot about all that. It was best left. Evie might even be the lucky one this time.

It was mind-blowing when Vix allowed herself to stop and think about it all, as she could never stop herself from doing if she were truthful. Will from the past, from 1805, coming back to haunt her thoughts, given dimension and life; then this Will, very much of today – a dealer, a gangster, and the person she had convinced herself she was actually looking for. Then there was the 'Will' Vix still really wanted so very much to find. 'Her' Will, what a joke! She smiled at her sheer stupidity and sank back into the comfort of the sofa. Vix decided then to meet this Stefan. This time she would get a full description. Ask more sensible questions. There just might be some millage in this one final chance to find him. And she wouldn't let Charlie put her off. She knew what she would almost certainly say.

"Not another Foreign student! Remember what happened last time."

Vix grimaced as she pictured Charlie's judgemental stare as she delivered those verbal blows. Then quickly dismissed the thought of just how right Charlie had been about her former husband: He had married her, robbed her and had Interpol onto her because he 'acted for alien government interests' and they presumed she may have done by sheer implication.

The police here had treated her as some sort of spy. Everything had been frozen, no money, no job in the end and very little self-respect. Vix still went cold at the way it had made her feel, hopeless and useless.

And yet, here she was, being stupid again, not letting that knowledge get in the way of putting this new life she had generated in jeopardy. She really didn't want to have to start all over again, even if it now seemed inevitable; she just could not let this rest.

But she needed someone with her. Rix. She would ask him.

Vix straightened up and pulled the laptop nearer to her.

"Stefan. Thanks for your response. Can we meet up tonight? Pick a bar by @ and suggest a time. V. Wren."

She sent the message to the stranger. If he replied, she would go. If possible, she would get Rix to meet her there as well. She wished that this lead, this Stefan, had not been a foreign student, Eastern European or Russian, she couldn't tell yet. All she knew is that it provoked even more anxiety, with images of Ash resurgent; she now wanted to move on and lead an uncomplicated life. To find Will and put to rest all mystery and strange associations that were becoming obsessions. Be normal, after this, she promised herself.

While Vix waited to hear, she decided to get her 'evidence' together – she thought that she had taken a photograph of Will, by the Victory, she was convinced of it, she just had to find the camera.

Vix searched around all the likely places and cursed the fact that she still lived out of so many boxes. When her sham of a marriage had ended she pretty much lost everything. Most of her things had been seized by the police investigating her husband to start with. The landlord had 'disposed' of her furniture and all those bits and pieces of a life that build up around you. In lieu of rent, and anything else he could think of. She didn't stand a chance, people like him just didn't care and why should they when nothing happened to stop them doing exactly as they wanted to. The experience had changed her, but she wouldn't let it destroy her, she was determined not to be afraid of her shadow, or anyone else's.

"Rix, I need a favour. Please get back. V." She decided to text him, avoid a protracted conversation, a liturgy of Rix's ills etc.

A message flagged up on the laptop:

"What's happened? Let me know after work. Charlie."

How to put this, she mused before straightening herself once again to inform Charlie that she had returned home to find an open window, previously always left closed, and a box empty of chocolates, but housing a brick!

She smiled, picturing Charlie's face. The eyebrows would certainly be raised, and this time with just cause. Vix just couldn't explain this one away.

The messenger flagged another email. Stefan had named his meeting place and time.

Vix's mobile throbbed: Rix. He'd agreed.

"That was that then, better confirm with both guys. We're off!" she proclaimed to the room as she stretched and paced the flat looking for the camera.

Outside, the posse of bike riders took to the street, doing as bid, doing their business as the workers from the offices, stores and the like trundled home to their regular lives having done theirs.

The tell-tale thin-limbed strides of the hooded ones darted around the streets, heads down, body taunt. The work of the streets had started. As they went on their way one rounder faced and muscular individual kept eyes on Vix's apartment block, watching and waiting.

Chapter 17

It was starting to get chilly as Vix approach the waterfront and she wished she had put more on. Thankfully, she had thought of the blue pashmina as a means of recognition. At least that was warmer than a red carnation, or whatever the tradition was. She felt a bit absurd.

People sauntered along in small groups, looking for the right place to start the evening; couples linked arms on their way to dinner and student-types stood smoking by the water's edge as disparate groups of chancing musicians played a concoction of conflicting styles. Vix was glad that it was busy.

She stopped and checked that it was the café-bar that they had agreed and looked at her watch. Bang on time. She made her way over to a table just inside the door.

"On your own again, woman? Looking for a man?" Rix's voice was suddenly behind her, he always made a point of being camp; he was not going to be ignored.

What a relief to hear that voice.

"Have you picked out which one he is?" he said with his usual spirited laugh.

"Haven't had a chance to yet. But, well, not him," she said, nodding to the large Chinese man who sat with a small coffee, two tables down, looking blank and uninterested in his surroundings.

"How do you know?" his question asked with a meaningful look.

"Now, Richard, be serious for just a moment, if you don't mind."

Rix straightened his back in the presence of her new-found authority and nodded his agreement.

"I just need you to be near-ish, keep an eye open, and not too obviously either; take a photo with your phone."

"Good idea, girl. I'll just mooch about the place, pop out for a cigarette, you know, look casual. We should have a signal. What? They always do in films."

"Now, Rix, we are not in a film, you…well, OK, you do have a point. I'll take this off or wave to you," she said, pulling at her pashmina.

Rix looked shocked at the suggestion, or perhaps at it, and a little disappointed by her suggestion.

"OK, but I'll put you on speed-dial and anyway, just shout if you need me, darling. We'll go with subtly."

Vix nodded and pushed him on his way as he waived at her.

Somehow, she felt Rix was just there for a night out as he weaved his way about the place, popping into a conversation or two and lingering when he shouldn't. Discretion and Rix did not go together. He was 'Extra'. She wasn't sure now what use he would actually be, but it was good to know somehow that he was there.

"I like your blue scarf. Are you Victoria Wren?"

Vix turned to face a man, in his 30s most probably, with a slight frame and poor-fitting unfashionable clothes.

"I am Stefan."

His speech was slow and deliberate, his English good, his accent soft. *Been here a while*, Vix thought.

"Yes. Thanks for coming. Please, sit down. Would you like a drink?"

"Yes, please, but I don't have big amounts of money on me."

"Don't worry, please, this one on me. Wine?"

He shrugged and nodded simultaneously and Vix left him with a shy and awkward smile; she wasn't sure how these things were meant to be. She had a flashback to Evie.

As she stood at the bar, Rix made his way towards her with indecent haste. *Christ, I think he's enjoying this*, was all she could think of as he almost ran at her, like a child at a party, full of fizz and unwanted energy.

"What's happened?"

"Nothing. I'm getting him a drink. Now, be more discreet," she breathed.

"You know that man?" Stefan asked when she returned.

"Sort of," she mouthed as she sipped her wine-spritzer and looked at the table. He was certainly alert.

"He runs like a girl."

Vix looked up immediately and wanted to laugh out loud, especially when she saw Stefan's uncomplicated expression; just the world as he saw it and he called it. Not that Rix would mind. He'd have something to say about Stefan's appearance for sure. But his remark somehow calmed her.

She had to stop it, focus and remind herself she was not there to get to know, let alone like him, he was not her friend. The most worrying part was he sounded so naively straightforward, like Ash, and she knew she had to keep that ghost hidden.

"Now, I tell you about Will."

Vix nodded and sat back in the chair, telling herself she needed to listen carefully and ask the right questions.

"I know him. I said to myself this when I read your request for information. He is friend of mine."

"How do I know that we are talking about the same person? I don't wish to appear rude but I've had that happen to me before."

Stefan stared back at her, he counted in his head, not too quick, slowly at first.

"I understand."

Vix coughed slightly, unsure where to go next.

"Do you have anything substantial to tell me, to help identify the Will I am interested in tracing?"

She was firm and precise, felt in control, pleased with herself as they talked.

"He is businessman. I know him because I have travelled around, worked many places, as student. He gives me work. Maybe no more, if he knows I talk to you."

Vix realised that he was staring at her with his hand open.

"Why do you want him?"

Stefan's questioning of her came as a slight shock and Vix was caught for an answer, but kept her composure. Stefan was easy to talk to and not intimidating. Vix thought she just might get somewhere this time.

"We met, lost contact and I understand that he has been trying to contact me as well. So, nothing in anyway sinister to worry about. I'm not after his money. And," she suddenly felt bolder, "I will give you money for your trouble if you can positively identify him to me or lead me to him in some way."

"Yes, I can."

Vix studied him as he drank his wine slowly. She wondered if her tension was palpable as he studied her back.

"Yes, go on," she encouraged eventually.

Stefan searched his pockets and produced a photograph. Vix noticed immediately, even from across the table, that it was him, the elusive Will.

She reached across instinctively, but he withdrew it from her reach.

"What's the problem?" she asked, searching his face, wondering just how straightforward he actually was.

"I am sorry, but I need money from you."

She was both impressed by his direct manner, his focus, and appalled by his greed, money lust or necessity? Everything had a price. That was his world. That is why he was there with her. All ticked over in her mind.

"How much?" Vix said abruptly.

"It depends, for what. You want to know much, more money. And you can have this picture."

"OK," Vix's throat started to feel dry. "You say you work for him."

Stefan nodded and waited as she sipped her drink to claim some precious thinking time. Everything needs to be clear, no mistakes, not anymore.

"Can you tell me anything more about Will?"

"Will, that is not his name really."

It was her turn to nod.

"I see. As I said, what can you tell me, where he lives, perhaps?"

"No. I don't know that. He lives in this place, then that, but mainly in London, I think. That is where I met him, first time."

Stefan sat back and looked around him. It felt odd sitting in the bar, drinking wine with this English woman; this attractive woman who looked so intently at him but who was not with him, was his enemy maybe. When he reached home and had money there would be more such woman wanting to drink and talk with him, maybe younger ones. He wanted to look Vix up and down then, but he would be discreet. He didn't consider her a beauty, but she had delicate features and fine skin, intelligent eyes as well, he thought. Stefan hoped that she was not too intelligent.

He didn't want that. He couldn't afford to tell her much, he was endangering his life and livelihood as it was. It had been the same ever since he had come to this country. These big men make use of you; they get you here, give you an address and some small-time job for a while. Then they use you. You mean nothing to them, a sewer rat, a worker bee if you are lucky, just an ant really, insignificant in their scheme of things.

He had come over with four others, straight to hotels. He had an 'aunt' come to pick him up because the work was not what he had expected. Stefan had been glad they didn't see the so-called 'aunt' who happened to be a six-foot-tall man in dark glasses on a dull day. The people had been nice enough to, even a nice girl there to be friendly with, more perhaps with time. But he did as he was told to and didn't look back. Auri had emailed his place to say good-bye when he was made to leave at night. That was a stupid mistake. Stefan had no intention of becoming sentimental. He had come for money. He stayed through fear. But not for that long now. He had his plan.

"I cannot stay with you, I will be seen."

Vix looked at him with alarm, at first she had seen someone after easy money, now she saw what she recognised as fear. But why? She still had not got any closer to actually being able to meet or contact Will herself, and Stefan's attitude now made the urgency for tangible action even greater.

"I'm convinced that you know him," she started. "I'm going to pay you for your trouble. But, I had expected more."

He looked at her blankly as she tried to fathom his eyes. She briefly thought that he had a reminiscent smell, it jogged her memory, but no more than that as they sat there summing each other up.

"I'd like to get in touch with him. I'd like to know more about him as well. All I know is that, well, you know him, because you have his picture."

"It was taken in Portsmouth," Stefan suddenly volunteered.

"Go on,"

"It was the wedding of an associate. You went."

He sat, looking straight-faced at her.

"As I say, I'm not doubting that you know Will, as I call him; I'm reassured by what you have just said. But how can you help me contact him again. I need answers to some things from him."

"I can take him a message, perhaps? I can't give you any contact for him." His jaw set, his deep-set eyes withdrew even more, their greyness almost like that of the pallor of his skin.

"Why? What are you afraid of, Stefan? What is he caught up in?"

Stefan tried to carefully consider all of his options. He couldn't expect much from her if he didn't tell her more. But he couldn't tell her. Not everything. He needed his livelihood. He needed his life.

"He is a big man in a world I know a little of, but not much. He has many friends but also enemies, I think. You should not want to know this man. But I will try to tell you, when he comes to Bristol again, if you want. I can do no more."

"Well, I had hoped for more. But I can see you are uncomfortable. That you are keeping something from me."

"Yes. Maybe I have to. Now, some expenses please."

Chapter 18

Charlie didn't know what to expect as she headed for the hospital. They had merely phoned to inform her that Ms Wren had been brought in unconscious late at night. A blow to the head.

Charlie thought for a moment and then made a call on her work mobile. They wouldn't like this one bit. She was glad Vix wasn't in range to hear the vituperative rage echoing in her head. She had been warned.

Charlie took a deep breath:

"I am going to ascertain what actually happened… Yes, myself and…what she knows, indeed."

She spoke slowly and calmly despite herself, enduring the interrogation she was being subjected to again on the other end of the phone.

"It is under control. I can assure you, yes… Calypso is fine as far as I know."

Charlie was inclined to listen, agree and comply with her instructions and left for the hospital at once. She realised it was getting out of hand and blamed herself for allowing it. Vix must be reined in for her own sake, if it wasn't too late.

"They told me she was stable when they phoned me. What's the situation now?" she demanded when she finally got seen at the desk on her arrival.

Characteristically, she knew very little after a curt explanation, it was the doctor, after all, who could really explain. Each had their roles and it was for Charlie to now wait with all the patience that she could muster. If only Vix had listened to her. Charlie wanted to tell her more, much more than she should, but she couldn't bring herself to do that, not here, not now. She had been told that the paranormal activity group had been pestering Stanley for more information, some nonsense about a road show and people being impressed by Vix's clarity. All this had to stop, should have been stopped. Now this!

Rix sat, holding his head; when was he going to learn? He felt rough. It was no good, there would be no work today. *Duvet day a necessity*, he murmured to himself as he curled up in bed.

Then he heard: Vix had been struck from behind at an ATM. He felt sicker still remembering just why he had been with her in the first place. She wouldn't blame him, surely?

He got dressed as fast as he could manage, still clutching his head, and in a pathetic voice, that needed no pretence this time, he phoned into the office.

"I'll be there as soon as, but.

"Yes, I've just heard…

"Yes, her friend was told to contact me straightaway, but I've had my head you know where.

"I thought I had better go to the hospital, yes, before coming in.

"Yes, we are very close. Thank you."

"Idiot," Rix said to himself as he finished his conversation with her on the desk at the office.

Interrogation, more like, he grumbled to himself before groping around for his clothes, trying to make the best of himself in the circumstances. Vix had no one, she needed him.

"I'll have to get a cab," he announced to the air with one hand on his brow theatrically despite no audience and it was a sudden flurry of action he immediately regretted.

"Resolve. And a lot of water, better not risk the milk," he said, putting his head in the fridge. "Fizz quietly," he whispered as he plopped the tablets in the glass of water.

Vix's three days in hospital, mainly for tests, they said, dragged despite the discomfort she was in. But it could have been worse with a very different ending.

This should have happened before, she told herself, allowing that cynical smile to form on her lips again, something she seemed prone to at the moment. *It just might have stopped me*, floated through her mind. Three days provided for quite a bit of reflection, between initial bouts of delirium and the round of pestering by a whole array of hospital staff: blood, X-ray, physio, the lot, especially painkillers which made her feel permanently tired anyway. Thinking wasn't always easy, and quite honestly she didn't want to dwell on some things either. Once again, she felt stupid. Particularly when she was around the 'oh-so-clever' Charlie.

During her stay, however, Vix had appreciated her; both Charlie, and to some extent, Rix, had been there for her. They had visited, asked the questions she couldn't and they had also told her some things she wished she had known earlier. They had not always appreciated that she was actually listening to them at times, despite being in what appeared to be a comatose state. It was a strange experience, physically being there and the mind somehow disconnected to that body, full of thoughts that had nothing to do with the prone self – laid out in the bed. She must have been worse than she thought. Not a great deal different to those regression tapes.

Vix certainly understood now why Charlie considered Dai Stanley such a Charlatan. He had toyed with the state of her mind without a clue.

"He has no idea what he's doing; he's got another young woman now. She believes that she met bloody Nelson. He has these little plays for voices, they play them as they hypnotise the person. I've seen it with my own eyes."

Vix had heard Charlie's cold and clear explaining of this to Rix, quite a bit about the techniques they employed too and she didn't shy away from saying what she thought of lecherous old Stanley. They were both oblivious it seemed to her body there in the bed still possessing ears, and understanding enough. She heard quite a bit from her bed from both of them as they delivered a cacophony of knowledge, ideas, advice, prejudice and speculation as they wiled away the hours by her side.

But they did not explain the likeness between what she had witnessed and what she had recalled. Why did she feel that she had met Will before?

She did, however, hear just what Charlie thought about her going along with the regression experiments in the first place, and she didn't hold back on that subject either. It was hurtful, hearing about herself, but she conceded that Charlie might have a point.

"She wanted another, virtual life, that's what they say. She also wanted a bit of drama in her life again, as if she hadn't had enough. The Will fixation has certainly provided that."

Charlie wasn't even that quiet or discreet and Vix wondered what she hadn't heard. What else was wrong with her?

"I believe that all this regression and obsession with finding Will has messed with her mind. Look at that drug dealer incident. That was horrific reading. Remember, she tried to find that particular Will as well."

"She even convinced herself that I knew him and had introduced them. I put her straight on that, poor love," Rix murmured. Unusually, he had been a good listener. Vix shuddered to think who he might be regaling all this to.

As for meeting up with that foreign student; he was obviously the one who attacked her, for money, according to them both. Case solved!

"She insisted on being alone with him," even Rix's whisper seemed loud.

"I've told you about the husband?"

"Yes, that was awful. Our Vix does get herself involved with some types, doesn't she? Mind you, I've seen a picture of this Will and he's very tasty in his wedding finery. I can see why she could get hooked there."

Vix didn't blame them. They were basically quite right. She went through all those similarities, or coincidences, in the experiences of that wedding day in Portsmouth by the Victory, both then, whatever truth that was, and the now version. She could still picture those people, so vividly, in her mind they were one and the same and no amount of logical talk from Charlie could completely dispel that. She was convinced that even Evie's likeness had been there, by the dock, in a red petticoat, waiting for a man. And then there was Will. She knew his likeness every time she closed her eyes.

Once home she would make contact with Stefan again, whatever they said, she didn't believe that he was guilty; she had given him £50 and he hadn't argued or asked for more. And no money had actually gone from her bank account. Neither of them had asked her about that, which surprised her. But there was no other certainty in all of this.

Vix appreciated just how fabulous Charlie had been when Ash had vanished from her life, but she could not go around suspecting every foreign student of being the same as him for Charlie's benefit. It was like listening to her parents.

This was dangerous stuff. That was what she needed to remember. Sensitivity to her feelings didn't enter into matters anymore after all.

"When you are feeling better, I'll take you around to Mother's for a nice cuppa." Rix emailed her from work. "Got to go, someone needs me, always the bloody same! Work, work, work."

"Do me another kindness as well, please contact Stefan, from your e-address. I want to meet him again."

Vix moved slowly towards the door as Charlie buzzed to come up, momentarily picturing the look on Rix's face when he received her message.

"It's me, I'm afraid,"

She wouldn't be annoyed with her, it wasn't important enough now, somehow. As always, at least Vix knew where she stood with Charlie.

"I'm going away for a few days. I've got to go to see my parents. Look, Vix, please believe me, these people are not quite as they seem, none of them. Not even your nice Eastern European guy. Still hurt, does it? Anyway, would you like to move into mine while I am gone?"

Charlie was her usual kind but abrupt self. Vix smiled but shook her head.

"I know your theories about Dai Stanley's regressions."

"It wasn't that I was alluding to, actually. I mean men like your Will, like this Stefan you met. They are involved in altogether more sinister things and you are now getting in the way. Christ, Vix, you've been hurt once, and really quite badly, please, believe me, this is dangerous territory."

Charlie was unusually pale by the time that she had finished and Vix believed her, she knew that Charlie spoke the truth, as she saw it. Perhaps, Charlie was also right that her mind had been affected. Vix felt annoyed by her friends candour, she knew she couldn't ignore her advice, she realised that the man was dangerous, but she wanted to know why, and why her.

"I know you might mean well, Charlie, but I'm not being scared off."

"You're mad. You don't know what you are getting yourself into."

"Stop interfering, Charlie. This is my life and I want to live it my way, however daft that appears to you, Rix or anyone else."

"Then this is a funny way to go about it, living, I mean! You haven't forgotten what they said at the hospital, surely." Charlie was not getting the response from Vix she wanted, or expected, so she decided to go further: "Did you notice anything about your flat when you came back home?"

"What on earth are you talking about now? I've thanked you, haven't I, for tidying up?"

"Yes, you did. But I didn't and nor did Rix, before you ask."

"What are you saying?" if possible Vix went even more transparent.

"When we visited, with every intention of tidying up it must be said, we were quite amazed by the place. You don't have to look like that, you're not the tidiest of people Vix, and this is a small space for all your stuff."

"I still don't know what you are saying."

"Someone had been in here. Everything was precisely put away, in the boxes over there for example, even the fridge was neat, and I had come prepared for that after."

But Vix wasn't listening anymore, she scanned the room as Charlie continued to indifferent ears. Yes, Charlie was right, she had not left her flat this neat. All the folders with the transcripts in were in one neat pile, the surface looked wiped down, the flat actually smelled fresh. Nothing rotting in the fridge or bread bin. No stains on the rug. As she looked she noticed more, all the tell-tale signs of a deep clean.

"I see," was all Vix could say.

Then she started to investigate the rest of her home with Charlie close at her heels.

Chapter 19

Rix gasped and darted back into the doorway of the Arms. He was convinced that he had seen him. The same hair, eyes, attitude, yes, and that strong profile. It was him.

Rix quickly lit a cigarette and moved out onto the street. He pulled his collar up with his free hand and kept a steady pace behind the man. He knew what to do, he had seen this sort of thing play out on the screen. He stopped once as if taking a call from his mobile, he didn't want to overtake him, after all, he was supposed to follow. Rix wanted to find out where he lived or at least something tangible to tell Vix. A mere suspected sighting was not enough. Not now. He had the scent, the taste for it.

A car pulled up close to the curb beside him, asking for directions. It made Rix jump and he was about to shrug them away with a few choice words when he noticed Stefan. Yes, the same guy, it was him, in the back and looking sheepish. Rix nearly reached for his mobile to check his photos, but knew he needed to keep his eyes focussed elsewhere, to remember what else he was meant to be doing: following Will. And he had disappeared around the corner.

Rix decided to keep walking, but not before he had tapped the car registration, or what he recalled of it, into his mobile. With a hasty look over his shoulder Rix clocked the car as it turned. He'd got it. Blue, big, a BMW M5; nice.

Rix looked ahead. There were two options as he turned the corner: either straight on, or over and left. He racked his brains trying to think what was down there. Then he tried to think where someone like Will would be going. Except he didn't know what Will was like, that was all very flimsy. Rix started to breathe too quickly. He felt suddenly quite warm. He looked down the road ahead, as far as he could make out, there was a young woman, a couple of guys, an older looking couple, cats fighting in the gutter, not much more. Certainly not Will.

Rix quickly crossed over the road and went left. As he went he texted Vix:

"I'm following your Man. And I've seen S. xx R."

He couldn't help but feel pleased with himself. He felt his heart beating faster.

This was quite exciting, he thought fleetingly, before catching his breath at his own recklessness. This was dangerous more like!

At the far end of the street he saw a man stop, step aside, as if for another to come out of some place, what he presumed was a shop doorway; he was sure that there were not any clubs or such like down there, although there seemed to be a bit of a, queue? Possibly a gathering? A meet-up. Rix couldn't quite see as the road dipped downhill slightly. As it twisted and the nearer he approached them, he could see more clearly. There were six men, all darkly dressed, all talking in hushed tones, a collective low murmur, and none of their words meant anything to his ears.

One of them turned and looked straight at him. He thumbed for his mobile in his pocket again, pressed, he started up a conversation with 118 118, stopped purposefully, looked deliberately at the numbers on the little shop fronts and continued his dialogue. He would put on a good act, he was sure.

"Yes, got in now, went the wrong way, won't be long," he hoped the person on the other end didn't freak. Give them something to talk about.

He turned abruptly, his walk turning nearly into a run by the time he was back on the main road.

"Thank God, the amateur dramatics are over," he said to himself with a large sigh.

"I need a drink," he concluded, this time out loud.

"I know a bar."

The voice was quiet and low but made Rix jump. He turned to see Stefan, the light from the shop doorway sign casting yellow light across his face. He was sure that it was him though, the same deep steely eyes, the same pallid complexion. A hundred times before at least, he reassured himself, he would have known exactly how to respond; this wasn't exactly an uncommon experience to be picked up in the street. But this was different. Rix was lost for words. That in itself would make for strange telling, let alone the old school cloak and dagger routine he was about. *Memo to self, don't do this again.*

"Yes, so do I. I'm on my way to one right now actually," he was pleased by his quick thinking.

He didn't like the way the light played on Stefan's teeth, they looked barred.

"I come," Stefan said, following Rix's faltering steps as he made his way across the road.

Rix slowed his pace a little when he noticed a few more people about him.

"You usually hang out around here?" he asked as Stefan caught up effortlessly with him.

"Sometimes."

"A man of few words, are we?"

Stefan just nodded.

"I've seen you before, when I was with my friend in town the other night, by the docks."

Stefan did not react and Rix wondered for a moment if he had the wrong person. But he was certain. He'd check his mobile when they reached the pub, go to the lavvy if necessary. He looked briefly at Stefan

"I don't suppose he'll be buying," he said to himself before a further study of Stefan to try to get his measure, but this time he attempted a smile to belie his thoughts.

The Arms was relatively empty when they arrived and Rix noted with some delight that he was the object of some attention, a few eyes swept over him as he stood at the bar.

Interesting, he thought.

"Here you are, I suppose you want me to buy you a drink," Rix said, sliding a lager towards Stefan as he nodded for another to the barman.

"Yes please. Good. Thank you."

"I think we have a mutual friend, Vix?"

He stared intently at Stefan as he spoke, who gave nothing away.

"I'm not so sure."

"We do. Did you know that she was attacked? After her date with someone, someone like you, actually."

Rix finished with a flourish. He was on form. He would dine out on this, he assured himself. He felt his confidence growing now he was on home turf.

"But not me. But, I know her. And I warn her. Now, she must listen."

"You had better tell me some more, I think. Why her? What has she done that she needs to be warned?"

"She knows the wrong people."

"Are you one of those people?" Rix sounded forceful and very serious.

Stefan supped his drink before answering as he noticed the change in tone.

"Well?" Rix demanded to the sudden sound of his mobile issuing *"Gimme, Gimme, Gimme"* in high volume across the bar.

"Get her," cackled across to him from the guys. Sometimes the uber-gay act could be a bore he decided, even if he had always courted it.

Rix raised a two-fingered salute and turned his back on the lot of them.

"Not now," was all that Stefan heard as Rix wandered off towards the outside door. He looked about him. They were eyeing him up and down, they would recognise him, they could tell.

As more music started with a blast of guitar reverberating against the glasses that lined the shelves, Stefan slid out through the side door by the 'Gents'.

Rix's eyes darted about the place on his return to the damp warmth of the pub. No Stefan. He had done a runner, gone. Rix was determined not to respond too much outwardly, he needed to keep calm, just sip his lager for a bit and wait.

Stefan didn't materialise from the toilets, and Rix noticed that the side door was noticeably ajar and wasn't sure what he should do next. He thought he was the man responsible for hurting Vix after all, so he had to do something. He needs to explore other connections too. However, a thought popped into his head that he did like the role of man to the rescue, it felt dangerous even as he relished the drama of the situation, the adrenalin rush, the excitement. Rix acknowledged that was what actually kept him going, nothing high-minded at all, which was the usual expectation of guys like him.

“I’ll join you for a bit, I can’t stay long, I’ve got some important business to conclude,” Rix called over as he joined Kai and the boys by the pool table.

He didn’t want them to think Stefan had left without him knowing where he was off to. No, he wouldn’t say too much at present, best keep them guessing what was up. Much more street-cred in that, although the thought occurred that he might need back up.

“Where’s your mate gone then?” a guy in the skinny jeans asked.

Rix didn’t know him, but noted he had a northern accent and was new around the Arms. *One to find out about later perhaps*, crossed his mind. He liked to know who was who as he regarded the Arms as his territory.

“I’m off now, actually. Tell you all about it some other time.”

Rix downed what was left of his lager, buttoned-up his jacket with its high red collar and left with a nod to the barman.

His mobile phone battery bleeped as he fiddled in his pocket for his cigarettes so he turned it off completely with a depressed grunt and made his way from the pub, carefully avoiding the mounted youth who slewed to a halt close by, picking up the packet that thudded to the ground before speeding off.

“Have you got a light?” a voice from behind called.

“Oh, hello,” Rix said, stopping abruptly and offering him his lighter, “what are doing around here again?”

Chapter 20

Vix sat and quietly sipped the tea that Mrs Rich had made for them.

"It's no trouble love," she reassured her as she put out her best cups and sauces. "Prince Albert," she told Vix, with a nod of satisfaction as the cat pressed around her legs, "Help yourself to a biscuit. Sorry I can't offer you anything else, I haven't felt like going out much."

Mrs Rich lowered herself gently into her chair with a small smile on her lips and melancholy eyes the colour of sultanas, soft and warm too, which made Vix want to weep all over again. She looked down and fondled the cat's marmalade fur.

"It was a lovely send-off though wasn't it, dear? He would have liked it, if that doesn't sound daft."

Mrs Rich went over the details of the funeral as they sat there during the last sunlight of the afternoon: the flower tributes, the lovely words from all those friends she hadn't known about, the candle vigil in the church. All those nice lively songs the young vicar had suggested. She particularly liked *'All things bright and beautiful'*, the one she had chosen herself, it reminded her of his school days, when he was her little Richie.

"So many tears," she muttered before dunking her nice biscuit into another cup of tea.

"Have you heard any more from the police?" Vix asked eventually.

"They've returned some of his things. They found his phone a good way off, flung up in the air I suppose, after the impact. They haven't traced the car. They seem to think that it was blue. Nothing else, hit and run most probably. Could have happened to anyone," she fondled the upturned ginger head of the cat as she spoke.

Vix's chest, her body, her heart, ached and not only because she had lost her friend Rix, who was someone not at all easily replaced; it hurt all the more because she felt his mother's devastation and was completely, compellingly, guilty for it all in her own mind. A mind that buzzed and throbbed with unanswered questions and feelings of remorse. Why had she involved him?

Remembering the small lonely figure of Mrs Rich in the chapel made her insides contract; she felt the mother's longing for her poor hurt child, and her sense of utter bewilderment.

"There was only ever us," she told Vix, looking into the distance, her eyes resting on Rix's photograph that stood on the sideboard; it was at least 20 years old and the warm eyes of the young man which looked out from the tortoise shell frames were uncomplicated, and so full of life. Mrs Rich smiled and returned to her cup of tea with a slow shake of her head.

Rix had told her himself how his mother had sent Mr Rich packing, and with a hot iron at his back. It was hard to imagine such an act of aggression from her now, but not perhaps an act of passion and protection. Mr Rich, never referred to as Dad, had one day, being the worse for drink, chosen to accuse Rix of horrible things, things his mother hadn't wanted to hear. He had then, in a real fit of temper, tried to take his belt off to his son. Mrs Rich had been ironing, it was in her hand, she forced it out of the wall and just she threw it. That was his last act in that household and he was gone by the end of the day, vanished completely from their lives.

Vix felt a lump rise in her throat recalling that evening with him, he so loved to talk and had such stories. Now that would never again. It was incomprehensible.

"Nice of those chaps to take care of things. He had a policy, so that helped. I don't have a lot you see, being a single parent so long."

"Is Mr Rich still around, in the area, somewhere?" Vix found herself asking, and felt immediately sorry at her on stupidity.

"Good gracious, no!"

Mrs Rich almost smiled at that moment, as if Vix had asked something so completely bizarre that it was beyond comprehension, the sort of thing a small child would come up with who doesn't understand the world. But Vix was getting to understand a little of the Rich's world.

"Wouldn't have let him know, even if I could. No, my Richie would not have wanted that. His father was a cruel man and well dear, we just didn't need him. More tea?"

"No thanks. I did want to ask you something else though."

"Yes, love, what is it?"

"Has anyone sorted out Rix's flat yet? Can I help?"

"Well, the landlord has been very understanding, he'll get rid of anything I don't want, but well, I haven't felt like going round there. It's funny I know, but I never went before, you see. It was his little world. And I don't want to go now."

Vix so wanted to help Mrs Rich, but she felt unsure how; she felt insincere because she knew that lurking beneath the offer of help was her own selfish need to find out if Rix had found anything out for her. Perhaps, he had stored the information. He could have left her something, anything, to go on. She knew it was secondary, but it might even help get whoever had killed him as his death was no accident. She knew that should have been uppermost in her thoughts and felt that nausea again.

Rix would leave such a gaping hole in all those lives he had touched, hers now certainly, but for poor Mrs Rich, it would be everlasting. It was all so bloody awful and she hated herself all over again.

Whatever was said, Vix was totally convinced that it wasn't any ordinary 'hit and run' accident and wanted to prove it. She wanted to check out his computer, his camera, his mobile anything, if Mrs Rich would let her. She felt wretched and awkward. But it had to be done.

"Mrs Rich, I need to gain entry to Rix's flat before it is cleared."

"Oh, if you need to dear, I'm sure that will be OK."

"But I don't want to intrude. If you want me to go with you, if it helps you, that is, that's all good. Well, what do you think?"

Mrs Rich sat back in her chair for a moment, before moving slowly to the sideboard. She pulled a multi-toned piece of ribbon out of the top drawer with keys attached to it.

"Here you are, dear. If you don't mind, I won't go. Perhaps, you would have a little sort out for me? Let me know what's what?"

"Naturally, of course. I'll let you know and then you can tell me what you want me to do with his things…"

All the way home, Vix felt the loss. Poor Rix. All he wanted was a good time. Fun. Now, he was dead. His poor mother bereft. The pain penetrated her.

She was also frightened.

If her theory was correct, Rix had been killed, murdered when he was on the trail of Will who he had been actually following that evening. There was also Stefan as well, who he had seen in a car. His messages were still on her phone. It was all there, could be pieced together but she felt anything but empowered, rather at a complete loss as she didn't know what to do with the information. She could only imagine what the police would say if she took it to them. They already had her down as some sort of nutter.

The knock on her head had been a warning, she could see that, and now this. Charlie had said that someone had broken into her flat again whilst she was in hospital, and she was right about that. Although nothing had gone, as far as Vix could tell, she should have treated that episode with greater suspicion, another warning. No one, nowhere, seemed safe.

Vix suddenly thought about Mrs Rich again, her obvious loneliness, not unlike her own, and felt pathetic, particularly as she felt the tears begin to swell. She so didn't want to go home. Just wanted not to be. Stop the world.

She considered going to Rix's place instead, but decided against it. If only Charlie had been back from her visit home.

"Excuse me, are you one of Dr Stanley's research group?"

Vix turned to see a petite young women with short blond hair and large, slightly bulbous blue eyes peering up at her through heavy black framed glasses. She didn't recognise her and was immediately on the defensive, before checking herself: the young woman had simply seen her regression tapes and had recognised her. She too was one of Dai Stanley's 'experiments'.

"Jenny," she said, pointing to herself, "I'm going there now, are you? It's great, isn't it? So exciting a feeling."

Vix phased out as Jenny continued, she had no intension of putting a foot in that place again to see Stanley, to let him mess further with her head, with all those thoughts of 1805, Will and all that, but she suddenly remembered something: Charlie kept a spare key in her drawer, in the little sweet tin with the cat on. She would get that and stay at Charlie's place. She would be safe there.

"I'll go with you if you're heading that way now, umm, Jenny?" she asked with as much of a smile as she could manage.

"Great, can I just say…"

Vix nodded her encouragement and Jenny kept talking.

Dai Stanley was lounging against the filing cabinet as they entered the main office, holding court with the temp.

"How wonderful, two delightful ladies," he enthused as Vix and little Jenny approached towards his encampment.

"Sorry to hear about that chap, Richard, by the way, Victoria, very sad business. I'm sure his colleagues will miss him."

Vix felt a little chastened considering her thoughts about him, she had to acknowledge that he seemed sincere.

"Yes, I'm really upset actually, I've only popped in to get something for Charlie."

"Happy to oblige."

"It's OK, I know where she keeps things," Vix smiled and headed for Charlie's desk in the other room, leaving Jenny with the tactile Dr S.

Opening the desk, she eventually found the little old cat tin amongst the paper clips, treasury tags and loose staples that sloshed about in the wide deep drawer, eventually fishing out the distinctive key. A large brown manila envelope had become pushed towards the back of the drawer and jammed as Vix tried to close it.

She pulled it out in an attempt to straighten it and close the drawer when she noticed her name on it in Charlie's unmistakable black ink Latinate scrawl.

"Found what you wanted?" Dai Stanley called light-heartedly while still seemingly pursuing his conversation with Jenny.

Eyes everywhere that man, Vix thought as she slid the envelope into her handbag and the key into her jeans pocket with a little pat to her side. She walked towards them with a muted smile and downcast eyes, on her way to Charlie's as soon as she could, no hanging around with them.

"Sorry," she said as the cat ran across her path, and then again, but with sarcasm, to the two youths in hoodies on small low bikes who peddled relentlessly fast past her in close proximity.

Chapter 21

Stefan jogged along, light fine rain filming what was visible of his face; past the restaurant, down along by the sweatshop, passing through the familiar streets and landmarks: he was going to leave.

He had decided to, there and then; he didn't want to see or hear anymore. No more youngsters pushing shit, doing shit; no little whores made of children, thrown to the wolves. No meow. No more dirty work.

Stefan suddenly realised his jog had become a run and that he was panting hard in the moist warm air. But no one noticed as he passed through the city.

He slowed, breathed deeply, looked around him. The shops had given way to houses, trees and narrow roads; he could hear the cars and smell the traffic, but further away, and no boys on bikes to skirt around the streets and sit in groups on corners. No one to recognise him from behind the net curtains or narrow blinds of these little houses that led him away, led him from what he had known of life in that city.

His hood was damp and clung to his head as he continued out and away from it all.

His run then became a walk, brisk and purposeful; he knew then where he was going and allowed a brief smile to touch his face.

They understood eventually, all of them did, that they were not free; they got you in and kept you down. He knew of no one who had escaped, returned home, become rich; just some stories.

But now he knew a place, somewhere he could go, hide, think maybe.

One of the guys that he had travelled with, Roman, had taken him to this place, his secret place. That had been before he went for good.

Stefan knew only the general direction with any clarity, but he felt his way and kept going, walking at a steady pace.

He saw the familiar short road, just after the bus stop, suddenly from the corner of his eye, as he went to cross. He quickly turned down it and started to jog once more. Yes, the little open green. He started to remember now, he could smell the river, hear the birds.

He crossed the path and eased into a walk again along beside the river. A man wearing earphones, passed with some open-palm gesture or wave as Stefan moved over for him. He looked around him then. It was deserted. Just the distant sound of moving traffic and the waves of voices greeting his ears from the backs of little terraced houses. He sighed and kept going.

Roman had brought him this way over a year before, but it was clear to him now as he moved on. He would continue on the path until he saw the little style that crossed over the flood plain by the river, where all that knot-weed grew.

Roman said it made people angry, Stefan recalled with a smile. He was happy because it was all familiar now, he knew the way.

A dog came bounding up to Stefan as he crossed by the field, the last time he had been there it had been full of wheat or barley, and dry. Now it was muddy from the recent downpours, and so was this dog, but he smiled broadly at the owner who tugged at the lead saying: "Good boy, Leo," to pull his pet away, with only the offer of an indulgent shrug to Stefan who envied the care given to the pet.

Ahead, he could see the first glimmer of the manmade pond, nearly a lake, he thought, boarded by greenery and young trees wrapped in white protectors at the bases, now going bare. The sturdy wooden benches that skirted the water had debris beneath them, Stella cans he noticed, abandoned bottles and carrier bags.

People, he thought fleetingly as he followed the path.

Some lights reflected from the depot, the other side of the pond and the road that ran along beside it, but there were no street lights, not here, and no houses to show the way either; Stefan liked that. It was beginning to darken, but he could see well enough. He was happy in the knowledge that the night-time crew would stick to the benches, to have their drinks or whatever in the reflected light. It made him feel safer.

He saw the sign then that he had been waiting for, carved into the hefty piece of wood: 'Community Orchard'.

The fruit would be gone from the trees now, no red pears this time. All of those berries would have been picked as well, either by the people or birds, may be. He remembered the blackberries and red currents, the gooseberries and sloes. That reminded him of home, so he picked up his pace, moving swiftly past the tall arbour of green oak, presented by somebody or other, the brass plague said, still harbouring a shine in the half light of the approaching night.

Then the first sign: 'No entry for Unauthorised Persons'. And a black hand in a red circle to force home the message. Yes, he knew that. And he knew something else too.

He followed the hedges that fringed the allotments; as he turned with the path Stefan saw another sign: 'Access for Plot Holders Only'. He smiled.

He could see the familiar little plots, some dug over now, all marked out in one way or another. Little huts sprung up, some had laid wooden pallets out as a kind of deck, an England flag fluttered, now turned pale pink and missing a clear 'E' he saw as the solar lamp lit up. He reminded himself to be steady, *Wait, be still.*

Stefan felt the corrugated fence that ran around the allotment boundary, looked over at the composter, the rain barrels, the sacks and sticks that lined the boundary. Canes with torn ribbon on them moved in the breeze that was mounting. It was a complete other world. It looked safe, homely, even in the half-light. He wanted to be inside, in one of those huts, maybe with that little windmill he could hear, twirling from its place just outside.

A big faded creamy-coloured notice read: 'Allotments Act 1922'.

Then something about lawful authority and £50 fine. Stefan shrugged and jumped over the fence.

He decided to walk calmly and slowly, as if very certain of where he was heading and for what purpose. The green painted shed got his attention. It looked nice, of course, but it didn't look used somehow, not like some with makeshift lean-to extensions and the ones with window frames merely leant up against the side.

He would make for the green one.

It was simple. He just took out his sharp-edged card of many uses, that was his all-purpose tool and removed the latch by undoing the screws, one at a time, nice and chunky, just right for his handy tool, taking the padlock with it.

Inside, the little window lit in some light so that he was able to make out the layout. It smelled clean somehow, that's all he could think, not garden-like as he thought it should do. There was a small table that folded down in the corner, next to that he saw metal hooks on the wall holding what looked like two chairs. He felt them, they were dry. He took them down and opened one up. A bit stiff, but the seat felt fine.

On the side there was a metal teapot with what seemed like twine around its handle, a small stove like you use when you go camping, Stefan had seen them in the shops. There was a kettle and some tins, two tin mugs, a bottle and a book on the side that was soft to the touch.

He fingered in his trouser pocket for his lighter and lit the gas burner. He shook the kettle, empty, then saw the bottle had water in it. He thought for a moment and went ahead, the bottle was sealed, it didn't smell of anything other than water, and he would boil it after all. He had it figured out.

Stefan shrugged and nodded with satisfaction at his luck; he would have a hot drink, even if it had to be water, but he guessed that there could be a teabag somewhere. He had a chair, two, he could put his feet up later, maybe. And he hadn't looked into the tins yet.

He smiled, coffee, dried milk, biscuits in wrappers. This was a good place.

Stefan sat with his hot drink and looked about his new home. On the back of the door hung a work coat, a mackintosh, a scarf; he reached forward to touch some thick leather gloves with material sides and in the corner he noticed a pair of dark rubber boots.

He could keep warm in them, especially with the thick socks that lined the boots, and with the gloves on, the coats over him. Yes, he felt pleased with his find. He felt safe just for a while. He knew he would need to be up and gone early in the morning, until he figured out who was who, when they came and went, all those important and vital details to someone like himself, in his position.

He put his head back and it rested on the shelf, pulling the other chair towards him, he made a sort of bed and stretched his legs.

He tried to sleep. But every time he started to drift off, he kept thinking. He saw that man, the one who had run around like a girl, the one who had bought him a beer, the one they had run down after he had tricked him. The man he had seen in the newspapers. 'Homophobic attack' the headline had said, then mentioned 'hit and run'.

The man that they had just murdered, just like the others too, all part of the business.

Chapter 22

Vix looked around Charlie's flat, so ordered and neat, but stylish, so unlike her own. Retro touches, like the cushions made from lovely old fabrics, Charlie liked her vintage, like the curved display case with its jazz-age feel, the artwork, it all said volumes about her, Vix thought, made a real statement.

Vix couldn't help but feel envious briefly of her friend having such wealthy and generous parents who had bought her this apartment, old-school purpose-built affair, spacious, well-positioned and her own. She reflected how kind they had been to her on her numerous trips to their cottage during holiday times or on a few snatched weekends. She hadn't always understood Charlie's mother, but she had always smiled a lot and pushed lots of eats her way.

Vix sometimes thought guiltily to herself that she had liked visiting because she liked them more than Charlie at times; even when they were young, Charlie had those domineering traits as well as being irritatingly clever.

She bolted the front door as so often instructed and made her way in to the fullness of the impeccably comfortable room.

Vix carefully drew back the long curtains that covered a whole wall of the sitting room, they were dark chocolate brown and discreetly embossed with a knot design, heavy and lush, giving the room a safe, protective feel. She noticed the designer print paper on the far wall and the Alessi bowl and corkscrew on the console table. It all made Vix feel special, cared for, looked after, and she thanked Charlie for that rather than dwell on envy.

Vix saw nothing untoward outside, nothing unexpected on the street that took her attention. All was well.

"Use the spare room," Charlie had told her, "it's all made up. Stay there until I get back, we'll do Rix's place together."

Vix sat on the sofa with a glass of Charlie's wine and put on the TV. She decided to watch the DVD already installed, until she saw what it was: another tape of her regression.

She was surprised at her, after all that Charlie had said about Dai Stanley and those para-psychologists working with him. What was that about?

She slumped back and took a sip of the soft red wine before seeking out the remote control; she was about to turn it off when something caught her eye. It made her stop so suddenly that her heart seemed to leap and she gasped as the wine fizzed in her nose and she forced a hand to her mouth to stop any spray escaping.

In front of her, on the screen, she heard herself, her body at least, describe, in the voice that possessed her, the attack on a women beside the dock.

"They found her, left for dead," the voice said.

"They carried her early that morning to her lodging house. The blood had been taken up by her hair, it hung around like matted hay, splattered red, deep now and congealing in clumps where it clung to her locks. She was, for certain, no longer a pretty sight; her cheeks drained, her eyes rolling as they carried her off. The women folk would clean her up, they would send for any medical help they could, be that barber or a man from the ship who had seen service with a doctor, an old wife who had wisdom, a quack. It had to be acknowledged by all that Quackery was everywhere. Those vagabonds talking of miasmas we couldn't see, in search of a quick profit, these piss-prophets, pedlars of nonsense. They claimed hypnotism could cure a person. I preferred the Chinese cabinet, those potions, those opiates as named, and those ways they had, they helped me more than the dirty goings-on of doctors of medicine that practised in these docklands. They were more likely to kill the girl than her attacker. On a ship you were safer, they were quicker, they wanted you alive. There is talk in many parts of the taking of bodies, the doctors wanting them for experimentations and all sorts of devilish tricks.

"I know that some of the men would go in search of the fiend that attacked the girl; a man like that could be from anywhere, go anywhere the ships were going or even just up country, but if he was about, they'd have him.

"Unless, perchance he was part of a gang, moving in, pushing their wares, not wanting folk to see over-much, or hear and tell. Then they might think on it a while. It's the way of things."

Vix shuddered. That now familiar voice was stilted and whispering as it spoke from her own mouth, but she heard every word and felt the girl's pain just as she had her own, when she had been struck and left unconscious in the street. She remembered the sound on the cobbles as her head dashed down on the ground. Vix remembered the sheer terror of it before nothing, complete nothing.

She sat quietly for a moment. Could she watch anymore? Her hands decided for her as she closed down the DVD player, stand-by as well, and took up the brown manila envelope with her name on it instead, blinking fiercely to discern what exactly was inside. Charlie had left her some sketches, amongst some other sheets of typed A4, with a clipped memo-sized piece of paper attached to them.

"Thought you might find these of interest," it read in her scrawl.

Vix carefully pulled out the first drawing. It was in charcoal and messy even though a sheet of flimsy see-through paper was attached to it. The eyes of the man in the drawing stared back at her, eyes that she knew, despite the smudging, they belonged to Stefan.

She hurriedly pulled out another picture. She gasped loudly at a drawing of a woman she knew without any hesitation to be Evie. The same hauteur, the same intense eyes, smoky grey and shuttered; the same distrust looked out at Vix.

She scrambled into the large envelope further, tearing at it in her haste, pulling out another missive from Charlie.

"These drawings were done by a Swedish woman, a doctor I believe, who produces drawings from pictures that present themselves to her when she has experienced or investigates regressions. Over to you, sweet!"

Vix was silent; she put her hands to her ears and buried her head into her chest. What on earth was she meant to make of these? It was getting too much to cope with, but cope she had to as this was not going away.

Vix dived into the package once more. There was another sketch. She looked at it carefully, this one needed scrutiny, it didn't jump out at her immediately, it was fuzzy and blurred more than the others, but it looked like someone she knew. Not Will, who she had been almost hoping for, but, well yes, it was Rix.

She reached for her mobile and texted Charlie:

"Please come home soon. I want to talk. We need to go to Rix's place. I want to talk to that Artist. x V."

Outside, a car screeched to a sudden halt, then another, as shouting erupted, dispersed across the road by the sound of bike wheels spinning, and the revving of an engine.

Vix sprung from her seat without another thought and pulled back the long plush drapes. The street was emptying of people and there were few other vehicles to be seen as she stood there looking out into the dark, trying to make out the scene and take in what was happening below; then she recognised him. Probably both of them as the street lamp crossed the drivers face as he dipped into his car. They certainly looked like the men that she had seen in the Arms on the night when she had first met Will, rushing through the crowded pub, forceful and arrogant in their combined strength. Just like those men chasing after Will down the road in Portsmouth. Completely oblivious to who or what else was happening around them, single-minded and brutal.

Vix tried to think carefully about their intentions, their body-language, as they stood speaking to each other in short harsh sentences before both getting into the dark blue car; they were tall broad men with heavy distinguished features and very threatening manners. Both had cropped hair, wore dark suits and had sharp intimidating stares as they looked up at her. She was convinced that they recognised her too, their looks to each other, even from the upstairs window of Charlie's living room, told her that as their eyes lingered over long up towards her.

Vix quickly started to pull the curtains together, what next? Automatically turning to look into the hall and check the bolted door, check everything with desperate eyes, before rushing back to finish closing the heavy curtains as the blue car with them inside turned and headed towards the bridge.

She stood for a moment and wondered about things. She tried to reason with herself: Did she know of them? Did they recognise her? Was it all just happening to her in her mind?

The cold dead eyes wouldn't leave her; she knew them and their ways now and that she would see them again. Rather than feeling fear, she felt nothing. It was all inevitable, maybe. Kismet – is that what they say?

Chapter 23

"Have you been here before?" Charlie asked Vix as they arrived at Rix's little flat on the fourth floor.

Vix shook her head and noted that despite the reason for their visit, Charlie could not help but pull faces at the décor, or state of the carpet, those mixed food smells that wafted up.

"A consequence of being up so high is it all just ended up smelling of cabbage in the end," she stated with a sigh, glad they had reached the top at last.

Vix thought it was probably locked into the fabric of the building over generations of disparate dwellers. All those lives behind all those doors, being censured now by Charlie. At least the thought was momentarily diverting.

"The key, you have brought it?" Charlie asserted with an arched stare in Vix's direction.

Vix merely nodded and smiled thinly. She was testing but Vix was glad to have Charlie back and with her, unlike poor Rix. She really did miss him, and it seemed so odd being here now that he was dead when she had never visited before. She understood why Mrs Rich didn't want to go. She wasn't sure if it helped to keep in contact with Mrs Rich, for both of them. It was still so raw.

But Vix was keen to get all the information she could about Rix's murder; Mrs Rich had been able to find out a few more details about her son's death than the police would tell her, and Vix was as convinced as ever that it was murder.

It became clear that although the impact of the car had killed Rix, he had also been stabbed, with bruising and the internal ruptures looking consistent with being kicked, repeatedly. Possibly carried out to some other place, not to where he had been found, after the apparent 'hit and run'. They also had a lead of sorts they had assured Mrs Rich.

Apparently Rix had been seen in the pub earlier that evening for a while, before leaving to return later, followed by a friend, someone they hadn't seen before. The young men in the pub said although that wasn't unusual, this one left, vanished out the side door, when Rix had stepped out to take a call out the front on the street.

A couple of them had seen the same guy on their way home, heading up the hill, jogging towards Queens Road.

"Let's see what we can find," Charlie pronounced, walking straight into the big open room.

There was a once grand old marble fireplace, mottled brown, and Rix had a gilded round mirror over it that reflected light from the large windows as it escaped through the wooden slatted blinds.

To one side of the fireplace, there were dark shelves stacked full with CDs, in alphabetical order, Vix noted, and lots of DVDs from all different eras with clashing covers, epitomising their genre or place in time. He had an eclectic mix, certainly an interesting taste, and it was all so well ordered. She went to the TV/DVD player and saw the abandoned cover of *'Avatar'* next to *'Love, Honour and Obey'* neatly packed away in its case, and smiled despite the uneasy feeling she was experiencing. Was this the right thing to do? Her mind kept churning, she needed to get answers.

A wardrobe with a papered back, dark with bright pop-art cats in various hues on it, projected along from the other alcove, dividing the large room up partially, allowing Rix to put his leather bed discreetly from view.

It was all organised and clutter free and very different to Mrs Rich's home, particularly the smart cream leather sofa with its cushions, a Union Jack flag design in pastels. Apart from the fluffy stuffed tufty-furred cat, curled in a ball, in repose on its arm. She could imagine him reclining on the sofa, but not with the cat somehow; it must have been a present from mother.

Charlie walked straight through to the only other rooms.

The kitchen, with a slope to the ceiling and an odd arrangement of cupboards and shelves, was certainly tidy, and big enough for a small breakfast bar and two shiny tall stalls. Vix looked affectionately at his line of designer products: tins, olive oil, biscotti, sea salt with herbs. All untouched, and Vix couldn't imagine him actually intending to use them. She imagined his approving eye tracing their contours though, as he prepared his evening meal for one. Then she really wanted to weep. She felt him there.

Everything seemed to have its place. A notice board with coloured pins in, ready to receive instructions, imaginative fridge magnets, some most obviously not bought for him by Mother, and it all still smelling so fresh. He must have had a plug in somewhere; Vix certainly knew that smell, almost a fragrance, it lingered here and in her memory for some reason.

"There's just a shower room off here and that's it," Charlie pointed, "not much of a challenge, Vix, we'll find things easily here, if there is anything to find. And he's so neat. So, what are we looking for?"

"Anything, everything, I don't know, Charlie. Look, Rix was murdered and I suppose, well, it could be that he knew something, and it could be here. Remember, he texted me that night and told me he had seen Will."

"Yes, and followed him, I know, and that Stefan guy you met up with," Charlie's expression was fierce, but Vix continued:

"I need just to have a look around, in case there is something he hadn't told me about, I mean, he could have seen him before and said nothing until he was sure or that he could follow him. Please, humour me, before they clear the flat."

Vix tried to finish in a slower, calmer manner and was eventually met an acquiescent nod from Charlie, who had gone unusually quiet.

Charlie walked back into the main bed sitting room and headed for Rix's little desk. His laptop was in the drawer and she smiled at her discovery before plugging it in, turning it on and pulling up a seat in front of the monitor.

"You should see this screen saver," she called through to Vix.

From the kitchen she noted the David Beckham underwear poster spread the width of the screen.

"Could have been worse," Vix said, smiling before returning to the notice board, Rix always made her smile.

The only thing pinned on it was the word 'Calypso'. What was that all about?

"I'm in," Charlie called eventually.

"That wasn't so hard."

"Not for me."

Charlie checked Rix's emails, which oddly kept coming despite him not being there to pick them up anymore; strange how it all just continued.

There didn't seem anything striking, not if you knew Rix that is. His documents looked interesting, but Charlie decided not to prey and dig too much at present, but just to concentrate on recent stuff only, things that appeared relevant. There were saved regression accounts, which didn't altogether surprise her, and a diary; he kept a log.

Charlie thought she should hesitate before looking into that, but continued, sticking to recent days, those immediately preceding his death. Rix had known more than she bargained for. If only he had listened to her.

"Vix, come here," she shouted over her shoulder as she shuffled some files around.

"Well what?" Vix asked, leaning over to look at the screen Charlie presented to her.

"Look, our Rix has made a note of the comings and goings of them, the men, Will, Stefan and some others, he says mostly youngsters, boys. Look here, basically all increasingly visible it seems over the last, yes, the last month or so. Well, well, he really should have said something. Maybe a lead? Who knows now?"

Charlie sat back in mid-sentence and looked up at Vix, who just kept staring at the screen.

"Then these are the men that killed him. Is that it?"

Vix said slowly, quietly, because one of those men was surely the Will that she had tried stupidly to pursue, and it had got Rix killed.

"I'll check his contacts list."

Charlie quickly turned from her, not choosing to cope with the deep and bitter sadness in Vix's eyes at that moment; a confused mixture of anger and desolation. It was painful and she was so full of regret, but they needed to focus. Charlie didn't want anyone else to get hurt, not on her watch. She noted 'Calypso' and scrolled down immediately.

"We don't give up, Vix, but we must be careful. Something isn't right, all this activity around here, and it's beyond our experience, but what I am sure about is that it isn't your fault."

"Why?" Vix uttered before rounding to face Charlie.

"Because these people are going to do whatever they want to do regardless of who is in their way, even Rix. You haven't made this happen. And anyway, if it wasn't him, you, it would be someone else. They are ruthless."

"I believe that you just might have said that to me before."

Vix picked up her bag.

"Let's go," she said running her fingers along the back of Rix's stuffed cat.

Charlie closed down the laptop and put it into the leather case at its side.

"I'll take this, Vix, see what else I can come across. I know people."

Charlie painstakingly packed it all away without looking at Vix. There were things on Rix's lists she hadn't quite expected and she smarted at her ignorance. It was one thing for Vix to feel guilty, but it didn't do for her.

"Charlie, you're quite good at all this detective lark stuff."

Vix tried to lighten her tone and Charlie raised her brows characteristically at her remark as they prepared to leave, Vix scanning the small flat, almost reluctant to break away from this last connection with poor Rix.

"Let's go for a coffee, I need to talk about something else."

Vix headed towards the door, scooping up a picture of Rix as she went.

"The guy's Will, sort the rest; they have Mrs Rich's approval," she said simply as they walked down the twisting flights of stairs with more eagerness than they had ascended them.

They walked towards Clifton in silence for a while, each preoccupied with different thoughts and feelings, until Vix grabbed Charlie's arm to stop her.

"Let's take a bench here for a minute."

Charlie nodded her accent reluctantly and they kicked away the first of the falling leaves from the old trees that lined the walkway.

"I like it around here, Charlie."

Vix received a look for that.

"And OK, well, before we get into the bustle of the café, I need to ask you about those sketches."

Vix studied Charlie for a moment as they sat down, trying to gage her feelings, which were as ever held close to her chest, before clambering in her oversized bag for the drawings produced by the medium.

Charlie eyed them all through quickly before shoving them back abruptly into Vix's hands.

"You know all I know," she said, her eyes scanning her surroundings and the people that passed them by.

Vix thought she was edgy.

"I recognise Evie. Do you know if she has been found, well?"

Charlie turned her attention to Vix suddenly, alarm quite clearly written across her face this time.

"You see Charlie, one of the drawings also looked like Rix and he's dead, isn't he."

"Vix, please, we know nothing about the doctor who produced these. 'Guessology' will not get us anywhere at this moment."

"I realise that, but you were able to find out things before all that information, newspaper cuttings, the lot. Any chance you've come across Evie?"

"Yes. I have."

Charlie paused, looking steadily at Vix whose challenging eyes grew larger, demanding without a blink to know more.

"Not called Evie anymore, Susan, I think. Yes, like Rix, same thing."

"Dead?" Vix stammered.

Charlie merely nodded and got up to walk on through the avenue of trees that led to the village.

"I'll do what I can. I might be able to find out more on the artist-doctor person too. Now, let's walk."

Vix followed, partially reassured that Charlie was taking this seriously, that she was willing to help find out what she could; she thought of Evie though and how it was all so wrong, crazy that this should be happening. Someone somewhere should do something and they just weren't. People used as commodities, traded for gain. Vix ached with the thought of it all, the old self-loathing creeping back up. She needed some of Charlie's assuredness, her certainty and clarity of thought.

The low light of autumn sun fell across the golden stone of the old buildings, with their brass letterboxes, bells and nameplates. A few leaves drifted about propelled by a slight wind, turned over by the whoosh of passing bikes and running children. They walked through to the Victorian Arcade and watched as the little shops started to close up, the theatrical jewellery and clashing Mexican fabrics put away, the furniture and bric-a-brac reclaimed from the walkway, and the great circular-end windows of the one-time winter garden shafting coloured rays across them all.

The last lingering smell of coffee and chatter of customers, animated and rapturous in turns at the end of a day, enveloped them, reaching out to them as they walked through the streets; but Vix walked in others worlds, detached from this reality, in a partial dream. She didn't feel placed in this modern urban setting. If it hadn't been for Charlie at her side, she might even have wondered if she was actually there and not merely walking amongst them unseen.

"I want to give you something, Vix."

Charlie handed her a small retro-styled compact, round green enamel, with a space for face powder and a little pad with a silk back. Vix stepped out of her detachment, focussed and was able to smile.

"What's this for? It's lovely."

"I saw it and thought of you. No, actually, I had a sort of turn out, whilst at home. Thought it was cute. Thought you might like it."

"Thank you, Charlie. And thanks for letting me stay at yours. I'll go back to my flat soon."

"No," Charlie held Vix by the arm, "no rush," she continued turning on that smile of hers that always disarmed.

"I didn't want to outstay my welcome."

"How could you possibly do that? Let's go in here."

Charlie pushed the long metal bar of the wide glass door to the café, pausing momentarily on the fresh hold.

"You will keep that compact with you, won't you?"

Vix was surprised by the more earnest manner Charlie had adopted so suddenly.

"You never know, Mother might miss it," she said with a big but somehow unconvincing grin this time that quickly dissolved as she pushed the compact back towards Vix.

"OK? Of course it is, how could you resist. Now, let's sit down."

"I thought that you might want me out, being so used to living alone, Charlie, and I did see an electric razor in the bedroom cupboard."

Charlie's face lit up, her cheeks flushed red as she gulped her coffee in sudden haste.

"Don't remind me," she said, putting her cup back on its saucer forcefully.

"I could happily forget that debacle," she continued and saw that Vix was looking at her in amusement and realised they were talking about something other than Rix and Will and all the rest that went with it. And they were laughing for the first time in ages.

"Never feel sorry for a man doing the right thing by his poorly wife."

"What?" Vix quizzed.

"He, Justin was his name, had left the wife only to return to take care of her because she had ME."

"That's good, isn't it?"

"Um. Actually, I did think so at first too, and I quite liked him being there a few days a week only. Then he pounced, came in, full sorrowful 'woe is me' mode, into my bedroom, wearing only a towel."

"And the next you knew it?"

"The next I knew? The next he knew, he was back in the hallway, with the towel following swiftly after. Before you ask, nothing of interest at all."

Their chairs rocked as their laughter soared, eliciting the smiles of those who sat nearest to them with their infectious high spirits, filling the air with a lightness of spirits that had surprised them both. This time the tears were joyful ones and Vix felt grounded again.

Chapter 24

"Hello, Johnny,"

Stefan nodded his head in a return greeting as he passed the old man. He was bemused at his new name and tried to think why this man from the allotment should call him by that name. He was also surprised. He hadn't been aware that he had become familiar. He always rose early, very early, hardly light and made his tea and cleared things up before he heard anyone about. He had never seen the owners of his little green shed home, nor smelt them or sensed they had been in there recently, in anyway. Yet he was familiar to this man, even if it was as 'Johnny', not Stefan. He reminded himself to be careful. He reprimanded himself that he was slipping.

As he looked at the sky, he could see that the weather was changing and not for the better. He cursed the man then as he knew he needed to re-think his hide out.

Why these oldies have to get up so bloody early, he didn't know. All he knew was that if that had been him, after years of work, of having to do or be someone somewhere, when they wanted you, he would choose his bed. A great big wide soft bed, with clean sheets smelling good, like the hot iron water his mother had used; and someone in it with him.

He thought about that little girl at the inn where he had worked. Maybe, if things had been different.

"Who knows," he said to himself as he crossed the allotments towards the gates.

"Have they found you?"

Stefan turned quickly to see the old man again walking towards him with a borrowed wheelbarrow, his eyes watering in the white-grey morning light.

"Sorry, what are you saying?" Stefan forced himself to ask the man.

“A couple of your sort, up on the high road, asked if I’d seen you.”

Stefan just kept staring at the man with his watery eyes.

“No offence, they sounded like you do, foreign. Of course your uncle’s lost a lot of that after all these years.”

Stefan squinted at the man, lost in his broad mutterings about accents and uncles. Then he felt panic grab his guts.

“Thank you, but, nothing to do with me. Sorry.”

“You’d recognise ’em, I’ll be bound. Tattoos to start with, not seen many like they had, might ’ave been in the forces, eh? Angry looking buggers.”

Stefan turned quickly out of the gate, running away from the main road, looking down.

“They showed a picture,” the man shouted after him before shuffling off with a shrug of the shoulders and nod of his greying head. “Typical,” he mouthed.

Stefan just kept running along the path, through the bare orchard and stripped fruit bushes, across to the pond where gulls had started to flock past the solid ridges of the turned growing land which flanked his steps until he ran out along by the river.

All he could hear was the man’s rattling voice in his head as he sped along. They had his picture. They were looking for him. Once again his guts knew what he dared not think on.

He knew them very well; he had betrayed them and Stefan had seen what they did to people like him. There was no escape. How could he go home now?

***

“The white slaves taken by the Ottomans always tried their luck when our ships came into port. They take our men here, like poor Will on his wedding day, press them into service, yet refuse others who risked death to join them in those mysterious shores, if it suited. Some made it though, as long as no harm was really done to our trade or need for friends in foreign parts. There were men from the north of Scandia, from the East towards Russia and from the lands overrun by the Turks. Odd to me how they left some to rule themselves in their conqueror’s name and the name of their God; with the eastern peoples, some souls were better off under that yoke than their own overlords. No wonder they took his God. The boys from the North African coast were the unpredictable ones. But for our part, there was gain to be made. We surely saved a good few souls who later would likely die, fighting alongside our own lads in battle.

"The world has ceased to make much sense to me, the more I know of it. I have become content enough; I sit here in the dockside rooms I've made my home and hope I live to see the girl, Lotte, reunited with her Will and her baby not made orphan. I can say with knowledge that I am blessed not to ride the waves again in this life…

"Thank you for doing that, dear. Yes, keep the thing, I don't do computers."

Mrs Rich's voice over the phone sounded croaky and distant and Vix pictured her sitting in her flat, with the wobbly lady-lamp next to her, her soft sultana eyes focussed on her boy, Richy, in the shiny frame.

The last time that Vix had visited she had thought how thin Mrs Rich had become, frail almost, small and bird-like, pecking at her biscuits. Previously, the table had groaned with cake and other goodies, all her Richy's favourites; a naughty pleasure they had shared.

"They were very thoughtful as well, dear. They dropped in to see me and showed me a receipt for everything they had sold. It's going to a charity. I left that to them. They said Richy would have approved."

She gave a little laugh then before sighing.

"They brought me a keepsake or two. I've got Calypso back."

Vix's ears pricked at that. She felt she ought to know what that was somehow. Why was Calypso familiar? Then she recalled that notice board in his flat. But what was it?

"I'd better go now dear, I've got a visitor, well, an old friend coming over for a cuppa. I might get the sherry out."

"That sounds good fun, Mrs R. Can I just ask, before you dash off, who, what, is Calypso?"

Mrs Rich laughed again, before sighing.

"I'm stroking it now dear, it's an old stuffed-looking Ships Cat. Richy had had it for years."

Vix remembered it on the small cream leather sofa in the flat. How odd. So, why was 'Calypso' written out and pinned onto his notice board? Just another of his eccentricities? She felt annoyed, there had to be a reason it was so prominent. Only he knew that now, of course.

"I'll let you get off then. Take care and I'll pop in to see you soon."

"Lovely, dear, I look forward to it. Now, you please take care."

As the phone went down, Vix felt that great pang of regret, of sadness. Poor Rix, he had wanted so much to be cast the hero. She hoped Mrs R hadn't read some of those things they had put in the newspapers about him, she would not have wanted some of her friends to see all that for sure.

Vix resumed packing a few of her things to take back home with her. Charlie, ever the organiser, was getting someone to help her with Rix's files, some computer expert; she'd be in a position to see if it provided any evidence to take to the police then hopefully. It had to be conclusive, names, dates, times. Anything concrete to ensure they would be taken seriously. As if their theory of a homophobic attack was not serious enough! She shuddered.

"Calypso. It was on R.s board. Any help? V."

Vix texted Charlie. It might mean something. Well, it might to Charlie. They might have been at school together, but Charlie had been way ahead. She had gone to LMH at Oxford, before 'burn-out' as she called it. Hence, the fairly low-key job at present, it grounded her in the 'real' world, she said, and gave her time to go home or travel, not to mention finish her thesis. Whatever that was about. Vix made a mental note to talk to Charlie about it at some point. Surely, a time would come when all this madness would subside, when it would no longer dominate her life so completely. It was beginning to define her, certainly her relationship with Charlie and it was all they seemed to talk about. All routes led back. And now 'Calypso' vexed her.

She looked at the small black case and decided that it was enough for now, she had things at home, after all. Charlie was against her returning just yet, so it was best to just go whilst Charlie as on one of her overnight trips. It would be easier that way. There was nothing stopping her coming back, it was a great apartment after all; she had got used to the relative luxury, the relative safety.

Vix tried to sort out her handbag, pulling stuff out she didn't know was there, then pushing bits back in, in case, before remembering to fish out her keys before they were lost again. Her fingers felt through the detritus that inhabited the corners of bags and she could feel the smooth rounded surface of the little compact which Charlie had, well, presented her with, because it had felt like that, something to be revered for some reason. It must have had meaning.

Vix smiled as she drew it out for inspection.

"I'll keep it on me, in case it gets scratched," she said out loud, as if to it outline its importance, whilst she continued sorting through, directing a nod of satisfaction to the oval mirror ahead of her as she pulled out the jangling bunch of keys.

"I will tuck you safely in this little pink bag." Vix nodded with momentary satisfaction and rose to go, bag on shoulder. "Good-bye for now."

She spoke with a grin and genuflected with a flourish to the charming empty apartment before she left and headed home.

Chapter 25

Vix stood talking to her neighbour haloed in sunshine outside the entrance to her block of flats, petting the over-lively little dog of Mrs Harvey's that darted around their legs as they spoke. It seemed like an age to Vix; she put down then hoisted up her case, and then let it go once again, before she tried once more to extract herself from the old woman's well-meaning if banal chatter accompanied as it was with the backdrop sound of noisy traffic. The goings on at the block and surrounding streets were just of no interest or relevance to her today, Vix had other matters on her mind, but she smiled all the same.

She eventually made her move, staying long enough only to be polite.

"I'm on my way in as well, dear. Truth is, I needed a rest, lovely though it was, talking to you."

Mrs Harvey gesticulated towards her bulging shopping trolley with a shy smile which, when broadened with hope by the look in Vix's soft eyes, moved her glasses off of her nose with a slight leap.

"Let me help," Vix heard herself saying, taking the trolley with one hand and putting her case back down on the entrance step with the other.

"I only noticed that the lift was out as I left and well, I still need my food and so do you, don't you Archy? Such a glorious day," she sighed.

Mrs Harvey continued to chatter as she followed after Vix through the large outer door. She patted the dog who circled around her solid legs, making it almost impossible for her to release him from his lead with her arthritic fingers. All the time, she smiled her contentment and it made Vix feel momentarily wistful, she never understood why her life always became so complicated.

"There you go, run on."

Vix smiled to herself as the little terrier dog did the only thing he had been told to do that day and sprinted off, up the stairs.

"Thank you, love, that's been a big help. Back now are you?"

Vix nodded as she pushed the ancient shopping trolley to a halt. She left Mrs Harvey fiddling for her keys in the worn brown leather handbag she always carried and attempted to run down the stairs to retrieve her case.

She could hear the phone ringing as she passed near to her own front door; she shrugged and would have continued, but Mrs Harvey called her back.

"Dear, I've heard that a lot recently," she nodded to indicate Vix's front door.

"Someone wants to get hold of you. It might be urgent. Here we are, I've found you," she said turning her attention away from the faithful brown bag to her door. "Hiding as usual," she chuckled as she pushed her door open.

She smiled as she let herself in, only beaten across the fresh hold by Archy.

"See you later," she called, still nodding her instructions for Vix to pick up her phone.

Vix sighed but acquiesced and pushed her way into the flat through a pile of envelopes, mostly brown or official looking, mixed with circulars; nothing noteworthy met her eye as she scrambled through it reaching breathlessly for the phone.

"Bugger," she said as it silenced to her touch, reaching quickly for her swinging shoulder bag and her mobile, just in case. She hadn't heard from her parents in a while, they would use the landline, her mind buzzed with 'who else' and she really wished Mrs Harvey had induced her to try to answer the bloody thing in the first place. She told herself to be firmer with people, more assertive.

Vix leant into the bedroom meaning to discard the annoying bag that she had hastily slung across her body and which irritated her as it bashed into her side with every move.

There was a smell in the air that caught her attention, she didn't recall it exactly, but she recognised it, but not from there, not from within her home, But where? Yet further irritation and then she remembered her discarded suitcase at the entrance.

"Hell, please be there," her face drained.

Vix threw down her mobile and propelled herself out and down, the low autumn sun blinding her as it radiated up the stairwell; as she reached the ground floor, it flooded in through the glass windows and the open door, so much so that her eyes were almost tight shut against the brilliance of it.

She headed towards the breeze that blew in through the opening she had left; as she neared what she knew to be the entrance she reached through towards the coolness in the hope of grabbing the worn strap or handle of her case. Vix felt nothing and saw nothing, just the silver-gold-yellow shadows, before blinking them away, searching for some shade in the street to locate her bag.

She stepped out further into a fug of sound and turned her back on the bright white sunlight into the clarity of the street before her.

It was gone. She glanced back into the hallway in the hope it had been moved further in there. Empty. She peered back into the street, back and fore, away from the glare and then into it again.

"Hey!" she screamed, almost choking, and sped towards a white van parked across the road, directly opposite the entrance. They were handling her bag, picking it up and going to sling it into the back, until her call stopped them. A young man turned and smiled at her, cocking his ear in her direction and shrugging his shoulders it appeared from what she could see through the passing traffic.

"It's mine, my case," she called out, stopping abruptly to avoid an overlarge youth on a small bike meandering the pavements, projecting her voice over and through him and a side-board brown Duster SUV.

"Easy lady," another cycling youth breathed with a brief stare as if she wasn't worth his time.

Vix dodged amongst the traffic as she ran across the road towards the van; the man was still smiling at her and holding her case aloft, neither in nor out. She took a breath and stepped towards him at the rear of the muddy vehicle.

"I'll take—" Vix didn't finish her sentence. With a sudden thrust, a rush of air, with strong hands from the two of them on her back, she was in the van. The case forgotten.

The doors banged closed, Vix skidded across the floor of the van, her head knocking the side. A projecting metal rib, that held a partition from the cab in place, stopped her abruptly, her side taking the sudden impact. She felt sick. She felt vacant, nothing making sense, just fear. She wanted to scream but nothing came.

She heard the church bells peel through the air as her hands sought out her head protectively; she looked up instinctively at the gap of light between the partition and the cab where the drivers sat. Drivers! Bastards, bloody villains!

The second church's bells went then. It was 12. That was all she knew. It was 12.

They cornered, she was being thrown around again in the large empty space until she wedged one foot into a metal rib and pushed against the side with the other one, her hands clinging to any ridges that she could locate, and any other skeleton parts she could grab or hold, before they tore at her fingers.

The van slowed its pace. The road surface jogged her around. She could hear them talking over the partition, but not what they said. Nothing really made sense.

Then: "50p," filtered up.

Coins were rustled out of pockets and clanked into something outside the opened window. She heard gulls and smelt the mud; they were crossing the bridge.

The van moved swiftly but haltingly, the road twisted and turned more than she ever remembered when she had driven herself across the road after the bridge. A sense of knowledge quickened Vix's reaction as she tried to ride the vehicle; it was one thing that she could try to do, however futile that was. It seemed the only response possible, open to her. What else was there, what could she do?

The van kept stopping. She took a deep breath, her heart pounding still, think, she pleaded with herself; lights, she guessed and swallowed hard.

She felt close to the pitted ground; she heard the whoosh of a bus with its sighing brakes when the driver opened his window again, she made out the very top of his fingers, discarding something briefly, before closing just as suddenly. They had stopped speaking.

The van continued, up and down, rise and fall, cornered, came to sudden halts and then sped off again. And all the time

Vix tried to picture it all, tried to imagine just where she was, despite being thrown again as the van picked up speed. Faster, more movement, more sliding, then indicators, they were pulling out, over changing lanes and then again, the familiar *'tick, tick'*.

Four lanes, she told herself, keep thinking, try to remember.

They were on the motorway.

Going west? she questioned quietly to the air.

Vix felt her heart jump. Yes, no big bends, and the brightness, the sun. Did it just feel like her old familiar route? Or was she being delusional now?

Don't think about what it means, she scolded herself.

"Just think!" she shouted, and then: "Where are you taking me!" out loud, at the top of her reduced voice, to the sound of a thud on the partition between them.

Vix tried to recall how long this would have taken her, if she had it right, about 30 minutes or so? This little half knowledge helped. It made her want to think, try to be rational, not scream or cry out. She needed some inner strength now more than ever.

She felt hot suddenly. Her mouth was dry. She ached from all the jostling. She rubbed her eyes; she wanted to see more than the little gap in the partition would show her and she felt herself start to tremble.

Thoughts like, *Why? Where? What are they going to do with me? To me!* it all cascaded through her mind. *Is this what had happened to Rix?*

But she knew how it felt to be taken by force, she reminded herself. After all, she had expressed it before, from within her own person, for the bridegroom Will. Now she really understood. She understood the fear of it all. Fear can make for restless souls. Vix closed her eyes at the thought.

"Where are you taking me!?" she screamed eventually.

The thud came and the van continued; Vix bit into her hand as the wind hit the sides and forced the van to sway as it moved over; she nursed her hand and then her aching head and tried to divert her thoughts to the road. She must keep thinking about the here and now.

The van slowed slightly, the indicator could be heard, were they changing lanes? Moving off the motorway? Certainly stopping momentarily before speeding off.

Vix cursed herself for discarding her mobile in the flat. She castigated herself for letting this…this abduction happen and in broad daylight; she had been told, she had been warned.

The van rattled over bumpy ground, they seemed to be cornering, more twists and turns, more bumps, and Vix felt it all. She also began to sense less noise, less traffic, just the two men muttering.

"Where are you taking me!" she screeched out towards them once again.

The familiar thud retorted on the partition.

After a short while they stopped. The door opened and a quick rush of air revived Vix. She could hear one of the men trudge across the ground, the noise of a gate, a sort of squeak and drag, as it opened and they drove on in, the van door catching a light wind and swinging shut. The smell of the earth, of water, of damp straw, the sound of horses audibly not far off, it all filtered into Vix; it felt of her childhood and her eyes welled up. *Keep strong*, she chanted, *keep alert.*

The gate dragged again, then with the clang of a latch it was fixed closed.

The van rattled on over the gravel and finally stopped.

Chapter 26

"Hello Charlie!" Dai Stanley exclaimed as she moved stealthily in and sat at her desk.

"Good trip?"

He smiled slyly at her, a long slow look from the comfort of his desk, his ample frame squashed into the chair, feet resting, one over the other, on the edge of a pile of papers.

"Working as hard as ever, I see."

Charlie's remark was acknowledged with a snort before his feet landed securely to the ground with a thud.

"Quite," he said without looking at her.

"Actually, I've been trying to pull together all these transcripts from the regression tapes; I wish people would put down what they heard, not what they thought they did. So much work."

His comments were met by a classic Charlie arched-brow stare that she hoped he wouldn't see.

"Never mind all that," she said turning towards him, catching him with a smile. "I might want a bit of help with a little project of my own. Hopefully I can count on you, Dai?"

"Of course, my dear," it came out long and slow with an accompanying nod of his round head.

Charlie swung her chair back to her desk, cutting across anything that Dai might have been going on to say. No one would have necessarily put the word 'sensitive' and Dai Stanley together, but for once he sensed her mood and remained silent.

But he wanted to think about something else, something he had been in the middle of when she had arrived. Think about the rather wonderful opportunity that had presented itself to him at breakfast for a sociable sort of working group, to help catalogue the transcripts; what a learning tool they could be. Yes, that was it. A 'learn-in', it had a ring to it, working on the project and making it enjoyable in the process, bonding. A small group could be selected, including little Fi; now there was a smasher. He allowed a little smile to cross his lips. Yes, he nodded, affirming his intention to make it very select, yes, that too would be agreed, couldn't have just anyone joining. *We could send out for pizza, bring wine, it might go on, after all, the entire evening. We might even adjourn to the Arms.* It all tumbled through his mind and his smile broadened, puffing out his florid jowls. Dai was pleased with the thought of it all, with himself.

He was rubbing rather self-satisfied hands down the lapels of a new hounds tooth check jacket when he heard Charlie speaking on her mobile. He could detect her body language as he turned, discern her tone change and then he noticed that look in her eyes.

"I understand," she said.

"Yes, of course you did the right thing. A terrible shock, I'm sure."

He stood up as quietly as he could.

"I'll come over.

"No, please, don't concern yourself about that.

"It's very good of you.

"Pardon?

"Oh, I see.

"I understand, yes, yes, the police will do all they can."

Charlie looked up into Dai's face as he approached, the dark face under the jocular visage apparent, and shook her head.

"Thank you, Mrs,

"Yes, Mrs Harvey.

"I'm on my way too.

"Bye for now,

"Yes, thank you, no problem.

"Yes, I'm quite sure there's some rational explanation for all this.

"Good-bye."

Charlie picked up her bag, pulled on her coat and patted Dai on the arm.

"That was Vix's neighbour," she said calmly, "apparently, Vix has…disappeared." She let the word escape her.

It was Dai's turn to look quizzically at Charlie.

"Details?" he asked.

"Mrs Harvey found the door to Vix's flat left wide open and her mobile ringing. She picked up my call. She is awaiting the police."

"Police?"

"Yes, she had already called them. Vix had also left her case in the street. I'm going over now."

Dai nodded; he was thinking however, not merely agreeing.

Charlie's eyes travelled across the corridor into Rix's old office as she grabbed her handbag and made her way out. She stopped: his old noticeboard, still there on the wall, left intact. In the middle of Rix's array of odd photos, cut-outs and missives was a square of white card with the word 'Calypso' printed in bold black capitals.

Charlie took in a deep intake of breath. She felt a little out of control, certainly a little out of her comfort zone, she liked to know all the angles before getting involved with things. Particularly when those things involved the death of innocents who merely got in the way. He had obviously got too close, found out too much, the fool.

"Keep me informed," Dai shouted after her.

Charlie nodded her head, threw him a wave, and without stopping again, made her way out of the building into an afternoon shower of rain and the whipped-up leaves which blew around her. What had been crisp, golden, rich, just yesterday had now become brown and sodden, lifeless. A shiver, a wave of fear passed through her, but she was afraid for Vix.

Upstairs, Dai Stanley made a phone call. His voice sounded almost its usual self again. Business tone on as he spoke, the Welsh lilt restrained.

"Yes, thought you would want to know, old chap."

"Yes, you should be very proud of her," he said as he gazed out into the changing atmosphere of the October afternoon.

The wind caught up. The great sails blew out as she turned; the great lady herself ahead of 'em and us, only imagining what it must be like to be caught up in this fever. If men be honest they will recoil at the thought of the gang, pushing, threatening and lashing out. First the whip hand, then the cosh to drag honest folk from their homes and rightful responsibilities, their rightful lives, as free men. Yet, you can hear song and cheers; cries carry across the sea and through the wind as it dances about the petticoat sails.

The great bow juts. And still you do not know and cannot tell, what inhabits a man's mind on such a journey. Which, of each one's life stories, will rise up in them? Course through their body, and swell the mind. Some will think of riches, some of freedom. Will thinks of his Lotte and his return. But we all know that the gang does not discriminate. Straight next to crooked. Fish 'n foul. Age no matter, nor character. Just numbers to swell the decks and holds most like. The Danes would not fight for us nor again us. England, she needs 'em all…

"You look wet through," Mrs Harvey pronounced as Charlie walked into Vix's flat.

"Charlie, is it?" she asked rising to greet her.

"Yes, thanks so much for waiting for me, very kind of you to call me."

"Not a problem," she said, walking through. "I put on the telly, hope that's OK?" Mrs Harvey spoke as if she was questioning herself not Charlie; it had not previously crossed her mind that it might not be appropriate to sit in someone else's home watching their television, when they had disappeared, possibly abducted, even dead. She shuddered and made for the remote control to close it down, a little red-faced by her own behaviour.

"That's better. Hoped for news… I've spoken to the police, they took a statement; I identified her case."

Mrs Harvey looked down.

"It's alright, I am here and I can take over. You go back to your flat and I will see if I can make any sense of it all, bound to be a sensible explanation for all this." Charlie's eyes flashed photographically as she panned the room, a small smile for Mrs Harvey still in place.

Chapter 27

"The West India Merchants in London, whose interests were indeed benefitted, appointed a deputation to express their thanks at our man's great and judicious exertions at driving the enemy. He tried to elude us, his people, when he reached Portsmouth, but elude us he could not. Folk knew the by-ways to the beach and collected there to see him. Many were in full tears, many knelt and blessed him as if sacred. England may have had its heroes back along, but none such as he, here, now. They loved Nelson 'cause he loved England, fervently. Us that had served, knew that his heart was as humane as it was fearless in doing his duty. They pushed forward as his barge passed, the dullards pointing bayonets at the populace until they were compelled to retreat as the people would not be debarred from seeing their hero. Nelson raised his hat to 'em, and they cheered amore. Now, we're to give that Villeneuve a drubbing."

***

As daylight broached, Vix looked out of the small multi-paned window of the room they had put her in. They hadn't spoken to her, just gestures, pointing and nodding to each other. Just locking the door, footsteps going down, then silence. There were two of them, although she heard other voices rising up from downstairs, all men, all talking in a language other than English which she thought might be Russian, then not, by turns, as she struggled to keep alert, awake, to listen. She felt lightheaded. She was hurt.

She traced the room for light as it got darker outside. No street lights here, just stars and, of course, the intermittent panning of light, spectrums from headlamps, with the sound of engines and turning wheels reverberating upwards to her little cell of a room. The vans, coming and going, the drivers' hushed voices rising up but largely inaudible to her anyway. Sounds and silence. Long silences. It was happening through a haze and Vix held the back of her head, as if better to hold in her thoughts. She needed to continue to think.

It was cold, damp and as the night settled in, she drew the meagre blanket up around her, despite its smell, wanting so much to sleep now, realising she had to be alert for what the morning might bring. But the shapes kept coming, faces known and unknown, darkness and light, voices as she clasped her eyes tight shut against the swathes that troubled her mind. She drifted until it all vanished again then lay open eyed to think about the here and now.

They hadn't hurt her too badly physically, not as much as they had scared the hell out of her, that was for sure; she would get over the bruises aches and scratches, but would she live?

Vix scolded herself for her lack of vigilance, she had been warned. She had known that something wasn't right, but she didn't understand why she had not reacted to the chain of events; her friend gets killed for Christ's sake and she still remained reckless. She wondered if she was actually going crazy. She saw Evie's knowing grey eyes, her weary stare. She traced events back in her mind, saw Rix, thought about Charlie, and felt sick. It all rolled around in her head as she fell in and out of some sort of slumber, sweaty and cold by turns, flushed face and numb fingers, dry throat and wet eyes.

Vix prayed for the morning light. Prayed for reason.

She looked out of the window to take in the immediate grounds, no other houses or anything. The drive leading up to the house, the paths about it that she could see, were all in a poor state, neglected. There were sheds, the brickwork crumbling in places, moss green like stains where a downpipes oozed or leaked, corrugated roofs and vans, like the one she had been bundled into, parked in front. It all looked shabby and isolated. There were some trees ahead in the distance and it was all quite flat. *Someone's house and yard once*, she thought.

Vix realised she didn't actually have a clue where she was, just that it wasn't too far from the city, but obviously far enough to be cut off from help, obscure enough for them to carry off whatever they were up to without anyone seeing or knowing. She now felt lost in every possible way.

She darted back from the window as she heard them outside, their voices rising up, their heavy boots on the gravel by the house. Vix wanted to see what they were up to, how many there were, think what she could do. Perhaps, they would all leave. Perhaps, she could get out of the room, try the window, have a go at the door. Her throat was dry and everything seemed to hurt as she straightened herself up against the wall beside the window.

Wait, she told herself.

The door pushed open as she stood there. The same two men, one behind the other, looking at her from the threshold, gesturing to her to sit on the narrow bed.

"Here, for you."

The second man was carrying a cardboard box as a make-do tray, like they had brought her breakfast.

"Tea," he said as if she wouldn't know.

Vix thanked them without thinking as she sat down. Perhaps, it was good they believed her to be so passive. There was no manual for this that she had come across. Charlie would have known what to do, say.

"We come back later, return with things, to help you."

Vix didn't really understand what he mouthed or what he meant, she didn't know what to do but wanted to act, do something. Her hand reached for the hot tea. She kept her eyes on the first one, nearest to her. She picked it up, slowly, held it high, as if to her mouth, her wrist twitched to the side.

"Steady," he said, halting the mug from falling, the tea from spilling out. "Hot!"

Vix instantly despised herself, what an idiot, pathetic! As if he would run off screaming if some tea went over him, and if he did, the other one would not have just bloody stood there. What was she to do?

She merely nodded and this time sipped the tea.

"What is this all about? Why me, why am I here?" she blurted out as the first burst of the hot liquid pulsated through her cold body.

They both shook their heads. Shrugged, went to leave.

"What if I need to, you know, go?"

They looked at each other.

"Call," the second man said. "I come with help, bucket."

With that, they left with a small laugh exchanged between them and a few words she couldn't understand.

She heard them go down, other voices came up, furniture scrape possibly and the slam of a solid old door. Footsteps across the front, the front door opening and an English voice. Talk and laughter.

The wind rattled at the old windows, Vix sat there just looking, all else outside was silent, including her thoughts. What was going on?

Her head ached and she cradled it before tracing every corner of her room, just one more time to stop herself screaming 'help'.

The door was ill-fitting. Only one chair and her bed. An old looking chest of drawers sat in one corner and she wondered who had lived here once, used this room as it was intended. There was that smell of damp earth and horses, one she knew so well from her childhood, when she had neared the place, but since then only the faint sounds of machinery and water, of goods being moved. And, that other smell. The air should have been fresh on the autumn evening breeze, but it wasn't.

Chapter 28

"They have her," Charlie said quietly into her mobile phone.

"I understand," the voice on the receiving end was equally controlled.

"I am going to see what I can do."

"Naturally," then, after a pause: "I hope you don't blame me for this."

"I do, actually. You should not have used her. It was your problem, you should have sorted it out yourself."

"But look, I was making progress…"

"Well, not anymore you're not, are you?"

"Keep me informed. There is no point discussing this further at the moment. Good-bye, Charlie."

Charlie looked at her mobile in disgust as he cut her off. She was angry with him, but she had to work with him. She would try and work this out. There was probably more knowledge of Operation Calypso out there that was not safe for anyone.

She walked to Vix's flat and stood outside for quite a while. The vans came and went. The kids on their bikes picked up the goods to deliver. She knew all that. She also knew the surrounding area very well. She knew there were plenty of places for things to happen, like processing what the kids delivered, and plenty of places to hide. The drugs market, the whole operation, was under their noses really. Police business, but also hers where it involved national security. They had to work together. Charlie needed a lead. And she needed to get Vix back alive.

***

"Hold steady, Will. There be land in sight and provisions for our fleet. No raising of colours, no salute, no mention in any gazette on the Rock; it all needs to be kept a secret."

But they will err long know of us a'right.

***

Vix banged on the back of the door, there was a slit in the wood and it echoed her thuds out onto the landing. No one came. She could hear them outside through the thin distorted panes of glass, hear their voices even if she couldn't understand what they said. They moved deliberately, on automatic, packing in the boxes, securing them, then back to the sheds for more. There were a number of them, mostly pale and thin looking men, miserable if anything but mostly expressionless, young without the vigour of youth. What it was all about she could only guess. Where had they all emerged from to end up here? Thoughts kept pounding away but they competed with her urgency to escape this nightmare world, she couldn't deal with both.

She walked back to the door, shaking her head and tried again. Nothing, not even as she kicked it and yelled. Over to the window again, the whole thing shaking as she knocked on it and hoped it would actually break.

At last, the one who had brought in the tea looked up and Vix beckoned him to come up, which he reluctantly decided to do after speaking with the other guy. She could not read their faces and in repose they appeared morose, if anything. She could not read them. This whole mess was outside her experience and she could not tell what they might do to her.

Vix felt a surge of panic as the door pushed in. *Keep it together. Get out of here somehow and look about. Something!*

"I want to go to the bathroom, myself, now, urgent."

He looked at her.

"Please," she hissed, apprehension fading as she leaned forward towards him. She felt outside herself. "I want to know why I am here," almost a shout despite her resolve to stay calm.

"Come," he said, grabbing her arm none too lightly.

The stairs were almost upon them, not much landing, a couple of doors on a short corridor to the left. Nothing on the walls, just old chip paper painted green, darker below the wooden rail. Nothing of any use to her.

He pushed her down the corridor, opened a door and indicated she could enter.

"I'm here," he said, pointing to the floor where his booted feet stood, just outside the door that he pushed her through. "Go, hurry," he grunted.

Vix closed the door and leant against it with a huge muffled sigh, she took in the room. The loo, yes, but water, thank heavens. No mirror on the wall above the basin, just a cabinet. She patted her body for the compact Charlie had given her and opened it with a gasp: what a mess she looked as well as felt.

It was his turn to bang on the door, followed with: "I come in now."

"Please, just a moment," Vix called back.

The bathroom was grubby, but a sanctuary; it couldn't have been more luxurious at that moment after a night on that bed, under that blanket in her cell. She needed to restore something of herself and to think. She opened the small cabinet on the wall before her – there were old hair grips, a pink plaster in a peeling wrapper, a wire handed comb with grey hairs still attached and some nail scissors which curved upwards. She had no idea what she could do with them but took them all the same.

As the handle turned, she flushed the thunder box toilet and walked towards the door, hiding her treasures.

"Thank you."

He stood aside and let her pass before prodding her shoulder to move her along faster.

"Can someone speak to me? What am I to you? Why all this?"

Vix realised that he wasn't listening, couldn't or wouldn't understand. Either way it made no odds, she was pushed back into the room and nearly landed on the bed.

"Ouch!" she banged her shins on its sides.

He shrugged his shoulders and slammed the door as he left. The key turned. She was once again left alone.

***

"She creaked as she rolled in the water as she moved her great body along. When a sole walked the decks at nightfall he was never alone, other soles followed in the sigh and groans of her timbers, in the movement beneath feet, in the tremor of the sides as you passed and in the flickering light. You felt the sweat and clamour, you breathed the fetid air and beating heart of those that had gone before. The night brings shadows and whisperings that travel with ee. Whosoever ee be."

Chapter 29

Charlie walked to the car park and waited until he arrived.

"You are late," she announced, opening the door of his blue Mercedes.

"But I have a very good reason, you will be pleased, I'm sure."

"Spit it out," she said, turning to him with sharp eyes. "Time is of the essence."

"I have heard that there is an operation that is about to abort a facility. They are moving on because of too much interference in their business affairs," he relayed as he drove off out of the city.

"Business men! Is that what they see themselves as, eh? Business men. Really?"

"Really. They sell commodities, even if they are people and drugs which destroy people and all the rest of it that you are about to churn out."

"Well, just get on with it then, please me: what do you have for me?" She gave him a quickly evaporating smile.

"Firstly, this is my operation," he said, cutting through it. "You know I've been undercover for a few years now and I can't have that blown, right?"

Charlie nodded and pointed to the road as he turned to look at her again.

"Well?"

"I have the location of a place that might be somewhere they could take her."

"Are you sure?"

He sighed, "No, Charlie, I might, that's all. But it is a lead and as you said, quite rightly, we got her into this, well, to a degree, and we certainly now need to get to her out, if we can. Anyway, it could be a spoiler for us."

It was Charlie's time for a big sigh. She wondered if she should have said quite so much to him before, but she stood by her remark that he had used Vix on that evening and when he had taken her to Portsmouth.

They drove on, quieter and faster as they got out onto the motorway, both knowing the sense of urgency the situation now called for, whoever was to blame.

"Are we going to take a look now?"

He nodded.

"Good, it's nearly 24 hours since they took Vix. She can tell them nothing, but it won't stop them from hurting her."

"My guess is that they are only wanting to protect their interests. She has got in the way, so, as things have turned out, let us hope they are too busy to bother with her right now."

Charlie looked at him and he felt it, despite not flinching.

"OK, OK," he retorted. "I'm not being condescending or anything, I know you are an experienced field agent, but just saying, there is hope. That's it. That is all."

"What you think, they might just disappear and leave her there? Really?" Her eyes shone as she counted herself down.

They sat in silence as the car made its way through large areas of open flatland, sparse houses dotted about as they drove on low roads with high banks, reed beds running alongside and no people to see them.

"Not the best terrain to go unnoticed," he ventured.

There was the occasional tree, some hedging near the ditches as they made their way over the man-made landscape of waterways, over crossroads and small bridges as they bisected it. The farmland had been turned over and some horses stood in heavy looking meadowland. It started to drizzle and looked bleak in the fading light.

"Charlie, is that you?"

She followed his eyes to her bag where her mobile, her work one, was pulsating.

"I'm actually getting a signal," she said opening the device, suddenly smiling. "I think Vix could be near here. The operation you talked about, listen, pull over."

He did as instructed, his eyes darting alternatively at her and into the mirror, always mindful, always on alert. Charlie noticed his agitation, he knew what he had done.

"I think they have her. It's the location you thought it would be and well, I slipped her a compact, it has a device. I have it, if not her."

"Best plan?" he asked as another car passed them.

"I don't think we should proceed now, at this moment."

"I told you they were on the move. Tomorrow might not do."

"I'm not talking about tomorrow. You need to get yourself in there, tonight, as soon as possible. I'll get someone out here. Let's see what we can do."

He said nothing, just turned the car around and headed towards the crossroads, back to the main roads.

"I'm dropping you off, Charlie, at a pub," he explained, pointing into the distance where she could just about make out a large old building. As she neared, she saw the thatched roof, the swinging sign, the wood smoke from the burner inside, all the detail she could to ground herself, stop her contemplating further for the moment just what the reality of the situation might mean for Vix. She could only hope that she could trust him this time to do the right thing.

"See you later," Charlie mouthed as she got out, her hood up against the rain and wind which blew up around her.

They were supposed to be on the same side, but doubt about him nagged at her: *What if his double life had compromised him?*

Chapter 30

Charlie pushed open the wide old door and made her way across the stone floor to the high wooden bar made for men long since gone to stand at, to lean on as they drank. A large shiny beer engine and porcelain pump handles decorated with old hunting scenes faced her as she waited, all eyes on her. Mostly men stood in muted familiar conversation, some contemplated their pints, a couple were seated on the elm settles which rounded the small space playing dominoes. All looked. She, of course, smiled to them all as she waited her turn.

"I'll have half of what he's got please, landlord," her clear tones announced. She sensed the small grins and saw the approving nods from those gathered around her, as they tried to get the measure of her.

"You waiting for someone?" the landlord asked congenially as he pulled her drink from the pump labelled 'Barn Owl'.

"Yes, but not sure when he will arrive. If anyone asks, I'll be," Charlie turned to scan the bar, "over there," she pointed through an archway, flashing one of her beaming smiles.

"That'll be all for ee now then," a statement as he took her money and winked at his regulars whilst turning to his till.

"There's a fire through there in the snug," a man with a flat checked cap pronounced, talking as he lifted his hat up and down, the two seemingly connected.

Charlie made her way through them, avoiding eye contact but keeping that smile, as she went in the direction of flickering light. Two English pointers, speckled black and white, sat before the open fire despite it spitting splinters at them, stirring only slightly as she sat at a small round copper topped table near them with her drink.

Charlie pulled a face as she sipped the top of the bitter he had given her, took in the old Cecil Audin prints, all dogs and horses everywhere and the sweet-sour smell of old spilled beer, then sat back in wait.

"You?" she announced about 20 minutes and just a couple more sips later.

"That's a nice way to greet me after I've managed to find you."

Charlie looked Dai Stanley up and down and couldn't quite believe it. Well, she might have guessed really, he did after all know her father so very well and Dad didn't do casual friendships.

"I'm a bit taken aback, that's all, Dai. Thank you for coming. You have been briefed?"

He nodded.

"Do you have a plan?"

"Yes, unless you gain-say it totally, my dear."

It was Charlie's time to quietly listen and agree, although under his casual veneer she could sense his unease and she felt it too.

"I think we had better continue this talk in the car," Charlie nodded, "I wasn't enjoying the drink much," she gestured that they should move.

As they left, Charlie briefly acknowledged the landlord.

"Who that be with ee?" rang in her ears as they went to exit.

"Down, Andrew!" a stocky, dark haired man with a big grin and loud voice called out to another of indeterminate age and crumpled appearance who stumbled towards her with cupped hands, to general laughter from the gathered ensemble of locals.

"Thank you, Landlord," Dai's commanding tones cut across them.

"Thank you, sir," the sage, stout landlord quieted them with his 'good-bye' as the old door closed behind them.

"Well, we gave them something to talk about."

"Not good in our game, Dai."

Charlie had to admit she still felt uneasy that they had sent Dai. Old school, past experience, sure but not exactly a field operative nowadays. But she told herself she had to listen to his plan. Charlie also noticed that he had dropped a lot of his usual jolly persona.

"I requested support to."

"Yes, I'm fully aware, my dear," he was authoritative.

"So?"

"So this is what we do: I go in, you get ready to get her out and away. You know that she cannot be allowed to scupper the covert operation in place by our colleagues."

"Nor do we wish to see her harmed in anyway, so your plan needs to be sound. Where is she?"

"In a farmhouse, apparently, not far from here, still getting a signal?"

Dai looked at her with just a little more intolerance than he had intended. Charlie checked her bag and nodded.

"So, let's cut to the chase, Stanley, what do we do? You walk up, knock on the door, ask for her, that kind of thing?"

"Exactly that. Apart from asking for her, that is."

Charlie looked momentarily taken aback, but nodded and acquiesced with the arch of her brows that it might work.

"I think I could be convincing enough as some silly old fool lost, looking for directions, something like that, do you?"

"I'm not quite sure that I should agree with that statement absolutely, but, I see what you are getting at. But, well, just be really convinced about what exactly you are going to say before any contact, for God's sake." Charlie could not completely hide her irritation from him, but he smiled all the same, someone needed to be calm at least.

"And, whilst you are knocking at the door, getting directions, to the pub or crossroads, whatever; what is my role in this plan of yours?"

Dai Stanley sighed deeply. He was too long in the tooth for all this really, but you never left the firm, not this one. *Yes,* he confirmed, *he would have his story straight, that was not the issue. How would Charlie locate Vix and get her out?* He took a bit of time to straighten things out in his mind, gesturing with his hands for her to be quiet when she attempted to speak.

"Right," he said eventually. "I will go in, talk, try and get them out to the car, do what I can, get their attention directed outside. Before I do that we will have a little reconnoitre if possible. I imagine at best you will locate that she is in there, still alive, inside, by that timely device of yours." He turned to look directly at Charlie. "I think it will not be possible to physically remove her."

"So I locate, probably not remove," she looked sharply at him, eyes stormy, lips hard pressed.

"Yes, definitely not remove, I can't envisage that happening and I think if we get that far, it will be an achievement, be realistic if you like, and we confirm to your contact. He will go in."

Charlie saw the logic of his plan, it was intel that they needed, before risking lives further, but she did not feel good about it – and did they have the time?

"It's difficult, when it's someone you know."

He started to speak but Charlie quietened him with a gesture now, and it was a finger to the mouth to be quiet.

She pointed from the car to the roadway ahead of the car park. Two large white transit vans had pulled up opposite each other on either side of the road. A man from the van on the nearside jumped out and dashed over to the driver in the opposite van, who had his head out of the window now.

They both watched in silence as the two men, joined by a third, remonstrated with each other at the road side, before a stocky young man, shouting something back at the other which they didn't hear properly or understand, suddenly returned to his vehicle before both drove off in convoy.

"I think we can say that is something to do with them, they are leaving their hide out."

Charlie agreed with a nod.

"Shall we proceed then, my dear?" Dai said, turning on the ignition with a steely eye on the road ahead.

"I'll direct. We will park up when we get near, close by, and you can rehearse your story, if you like."

"I don't like, my dear. You plan yours in case you are seen. Much better all round, I'd say."

Charlie eyed him with a sideward glance, but nodded her head and remained focussed on directing him.

The drizzling rain still persisted and it was getting darker but Charlie could only focus on the possibility that it was Vix that held onto the compact, had activated it when she had opened it. She wasn't exactly sure why they had targeted and held her in particular, but they would in all likely hood dispose of her before they left, and they seemed to be on the move all right. It fitted from what she knew, she was convinced of that.

Her mobile flashed a text; it was Jakob. He was heading back, should only be contacted to give whereabouts of target once in place. Confirm. It was his last call before moving in then.

"Confirm, heading there now. Out." she texted back.

"Put your foot down, Stanley," she said cheerily.

Dai nodded with a grin: "Back in the day, I'll have you know."

Chapter 31

"The Mediterranean fleet welcomed him with as much love and anticipation as those he had left in Portsmouth, with tears and blessings aplenty. The eyes of his fleet, the frigates, soon had us those provisions meant for France, seized they were, which forced them to venture out. He had his plans. Cut off the enemy ships at the centre, break through; no captain can do wrong in his eyes if he places himself alongside the enemy of England. And before the battle, his last order would surely be to have the names of those that served, navy or marine, for the patriotic fund to help maimed or those with loved ones that would be in need of it should they not return. That those that know say is his way. Though none thought overlong on that prospect. There was much to be ready for."

***

Vix looked out of her little window panes, seeing through the drizzle to where the vans were being stacked. She tried to focus, her mind busy elsewhere, in that other place, the only place it wanted to be now, to escape to. Her mind echoed with others thoughts which she couldn't own but wanted to be enveloped in now that the alternative was her own capture and torment.

Only two left now. How long had she drifted? They continued to shout, raise voices to each other, the tones were harsh, aggressive and their body language reinforced their shared animosity. Something wasn't right between them or what they were about to embark upon. Apart from the voices of the past, Vix had little else to ponder on in her prison room, she even smiled at the fact that her fate was starting to resemble the captives on the ship. Little people used in the game where others had the power to pull the strings.

She had also exhausted her self-suggestions about exactly what action she could take to help herself. If it really came to it, if she really thought that they were…going to finish her, then she'd do whatever she could. It wasn't exactly a comforting thought. No one had come near her, or had spoken to her; they had been more preoccupied with whatever they were up to than with her, who they had taken. Perhaps, they realised it was a mistake. Perhaps, perhaps, her mind throbbed with them. Her body ached as well now too, she felt cold and hungry, but that paled into insignificance against the mental fatigue. The continuing agony of: *What can I do?*

A car drew up, over the gravel and stopped abruptly. A door swung open and was slammed shut. Vix peered out again. A tall looking man in a hooded jacket was walking towards those nearest the house, possibly the ones who had picked her up, they didn't seem to do much else. They weren't the worker bees.

Vix could hear quite a lot of talking – the man who had just arrived was English. She craned to hear, hoping to find out what was going on, but nothing made much sense. She heard them laughing, saw the English guy throw back his head, slap one of her jailers on the back and then saw his hood fall back, saw his profile then his eyes as he looked up at her. She gasped and almost fell back. It was him. It was Will.

"Who's that?" she heard him say, loudly and audible through the rain, she saw him pointing up at her standing at the window before turning his back to her in a huddle with the men.

Vix didn't know what to think because she couldn't feel, she was stunned, in shock all over again. She started breathing heavily, her chest rising up and down, too quickly, not right, slow slow, please, slow, steady, her hands on her throat and then her chest. She closed her eyes as the door pushed open, wide in that usual sweep, as if affirming their power, their control. She fixed them with her eyes, still holding her chest.

"This is she."

"What's that all about, then? Eh?" Will asked quizzing them both.

"Jakob, you know, poking the nose where not wanted. She is trouble for us."

Vix stared at them: "Jakob?" she sneered, *not Will then. Bloody liar.*

"You guys do as you think best. But just remember, we don't want anything leading to us. Who hired this place?"

The two men looked at each other and shrugged and Will walked them to the threshold to talk.

"It's not our job. That is taken care of. We do what needed with the merchandise, in and out," they spoke in quieter tones. "Well, the people part will need to be diverted elsewhere. Need to set up elsewhere too. There has been a complaint about your farm workers."

"What do you mean?"

"The police have a special unit if people are suspicious of foreign workers. That sort of thing. One topped himself, I heard." Will did the movement, imaginary rope and half-tilted head to knowing nods. "We don't need attention."

"That's why we take her. She has been to police, said about one of our guys, him missing now."

Will walked back fully into the room, they followed his lead, then crossed over directly to her.

"Hope you didn't hear any of that," he said, staring at her intently.

She just shook her head, the rest of her remaining very, very still, even the heaving chest quietened.

He made a move to grab her arm, looked at her with a sudden menace that frightened her until he pressed her hand and turned abruptly.

"You like?"

"Not my type," he answered coolly and they all laughed, casting eyes back at her.

"I think you have mistaken me," Vix called out suddenly, "got the wrong person or something," clenching her fist until the paper he had pressed into her hand cut into her.

All three looked at the other and shot her a different sort of look, as if she was beyond their belief and not just an unpleasant smell under their nose as usual.

"We'll look into it. Come on fellas, let's go get some vodka downstairs for me."

They laughed again and went to go, but not before the speaking half of her captive duo pointed his finger at her to get away from the window, then 'sit', like you would to a dog.

Vix sat. They left, but she didn't hear the door key turn. She opened her hand and saw the small piece of paper, almost lodged there where Will had pushed it deftly into her palm. She waited as she listened to the squeak of the treads as they went downstairs. Their voices fading to inaudible peaks and lows, the sound of activity in the room below just discernible. Then Vix very carefully unfurled the paper he had given her, her fingers stiff and almost numb, but she needed to be diligent. She couldn't rip it, she had to be careful, it was the only glimmer of hope she had had.

"Window."

Vix read it again and again. She still despaired for her safety, but at least there was some sort of hope somehow now. Although she wondered why she should put her trust in him after all that had happened. Will, now Jakob. What was her alternative?

***

"I don't fight for England's glory, neither for the love of a lord, history can say as it likes, I fight my fear for me. I fight to survive. So stir me to it with all the talk of valour, glory and more; watch me get ready for war, stand shoulder to shoulder with my kind in the hope of a life for another time."

Chapter 32

"You alright there?"

Charlie looked up to see that the woman nearing her on the horse was talking to her, looking down quizzically from beneath the brim of her riding hat. *She fitted*, Charlie thought, *no need to be concerned about her.* She remembered village life, she just needed to reassure, to fit.

"Yes, thank you. Just having a nose," she called up affably.

"Heard it was for sale, about time," she tossed her head towards the house with a knowing look that Charlie responded to.

"For sale, oh, not sure it's actually on the market yet, so better keep it quiet," Charlie smiled broadly and then in almost hushed conspiratorial tone, mouthed: "Love to know more about it. Looks like it's been empty a while. No ghosts, I hope!"

They both laughed as Charlie's eyes urged the woman on.

"No, nothing like that. Just, well, end of the line you might say for that old family around here. Old chap in a home, might even have passed, no one rightly knows. Community isn't what it once was."

"Well, we were interested in a project, but looks like they might have builders in there, from the vans at the front that I could see." Charlie had crossed closer to the chestnut, quietly stroking her, patting her nose before she snorted her hand away, tossing her head.

"Heavens no. That's the crew they rented it out to. Foreigners, I've heard. Some sort of business or other. I don't pay much heed. They don't trouble us."

Charlie nodded understandingly, still befriending the horse affectionately.

"You have made me curious. I wouldn't mind getting a closer look but, well, not sure I want to intrude on those foreigners, don't know what the business is!" Charlie's eyes were mischievous now.

"Never thought of that!" the woman guffawed back. "What I would say is that if you go over there, that way."

Charlie followed her pointing finger as it travelled over the road to the opposite side, round a slight bend in the hedges surrounding the place.

"I see," she said with a discreet nod.

"Well, you can look through, see a fair bit now that the leaves are thinning and all. Take a sneaky peak, why not. But, I wouldn't hang about as it looks like we have got some more rain due."

Charlie put up her hand in acknowledgment as the woman turned her heels and with the briefest of scans to the road, clicked on her encouragement to the chestnut to ride on.

"Good luck," she called as she trotted off at a pace, leaving Charlie to wave limply until she was safely out of sight.

Charlie stealthily made her way over the road to the property's perimeter and as the woman had indicated, saw through to the back of the house. No lights were on. She could hear voices, they were foreign tongued voices and they were outside; she saw small shafts of light appearing then going, as if with the opening and shutting doors. Movement.

She scanned the hedges and decided on a way through; pulling her coat close into her frame she squeezed in, her bag hanging at the front of her, making her sway slightly as it swung to the right, nearly over balancing with a post saving her. She got through, all intact, feet on firm ground despite her heels and the drizzle. It was getting darker but all was still visible. Which meant she would be too. She took out her mobile as stealthily as she could and texted to Dai where she was. He needed to get a move on. Working with him did not inspire her confidence. She took a deep breath and stepped forward.

She approached the rear of the main building where an outbuilding jutted out from the old solid square of a house by the look of things. Charlie weighed up two courses of action: Go in or snoop? Her mind was made up for her by screeching tyres and crunching gravel at the front which caused the entrance door to bang open and a cacophony of voices and remonstrations erupt.

"Private property!" a loud shout went out in broken English.

Then:

"Go. Move!"

"No worries, no cause for alarm, sorry to disturb, a bit lost!"

Charlie recognised that voice and cringed slightly: Dai was actually doing what he had said he would, and it didn't lessen her apprehension in his plan, not in the cold light of things. She pictured his grin and smoothing hands spreading out as he stooped his head slightly to one side before them.

"Do you think you could be of any assistance?" Dai waived his turned off mobile phone, before slipping it into his overcoat pocket, pressing it on.

"What you say? What he want?" they turned towards Will who had now walked out onto the drive.

"Leave it with me," their Jakob said, and they nodded agreement with a smirk here and a shrug there.

"What seems to be the problem?" he asked Dai, who had noticed the indolent attitude of the men and smelt alcohol as well as the fumes of the merchandise they had been stacking.

"Sorry to be a nuisance. Only, I'm lost, well, just a tad, and no wretched charge left on my mobile phone – hardly use the thing! Anyway, I was hoping to make a call so my partner could let me know where to meet. Need to be discreet you see. Say no more! I seem, however, to have upset your, your?"

"Colleagues," Will interjected as Dai faltered, spinning it out, smiling, stumbling, gesticulating until Will fixed him with a look that chastened him in bit.

"I see, yes, well, please convey I meant no harm. Being a bit covert myself, not that I'm suggesting."

"I should hope not," Will pronounced with a hint of aggression in his tone to appease the men, and caution Stanley with his theatricals.

"No, no. So, the fact of the matter is, I need to make contact with, well, let's just say, a friend."

Charlie could hear Dai's voice, visualise the scene, and found herself hoping he wasn't winking at that particular point.

"Hold on a minute."

There was a brief pause as Will turned into the porch to talk to the men.

"Here," he said, pushing a mobile in Dai's gloved hand.

"Just a moment," he said pushing it back, whilst he pedantically removed them.

Will walked him slowly back from the porch, holding up the mobile as if searching for a good signal.

"Here you go. Looks OK to me. Make your call."

"I will, thank you so very much. Very obliged. We know how ladies can be."

"I should get a move on with it as the sky's turning, wind coming up I would guess, and I'd like to get out of this wet."

As Will talked, he gestured to the sky, his hand moving towards the house, throwing a glance upwards then back directly to Dai Stanley.

"Ah, yes, naturally. Thank you, I'll just turn my back," Dai padded off, talking in elaborately hushed tones.

Will walked back to the guys who stood smoking by the porch, eyeing everything. He raised his eyebrows and gestured with his hands, down low between his legs, mouthing 'Wanker' to them even though the gesture was enough and international.

"We need to keep locals sweet… No attention. Cool?" he spoke in a whisper, with the desired result. They trusted him. He was their friend by now and he knew such things. Yes, it was cool with them.

"So very kind," Dai said, walking back towards them with the mobile phone.

"Now you go!"

Will took the mobile before they said or did anything further – Dai was trying his luck.

"No worries. Perhaps, you could move your car, we are expecting deliveries, business. I presume you were planning on doing that, anyway, I think my colleagues made themselves clear."

"Indeed," Dai bowed his head in acknowledgment and walked purposefully back to his car, his mobile throbbing in his breast pocket.

He had seen her alright. And what's more, she had seen him. Now, where was Charlie?

Dai drove away just far enough to get out of sight. He needed to give some thought to this lot. They didn't want fatalities. They could not risk a civilian. They could not risk the covert operation that Will had put two years into. Yes, he needs to think and take counsel.

Chapter 33

Vix had understood that Will was playing a double-handed game, she knew to them he was Jakob, but who he really was, she could only second-guess. Then what about Dai Stanley, what could he have to do with all this? Then the cryptic message 'Window', what was she supposed to do with that? He had wanted her to be seen, and to see?

She stood transfixed on the window. Their business had commenced again, more movement, more loading and more of that tell-tale stench, more zombie workers. They grew and distributed cannabis, they were some kind of gang, brought in for the purpose, whether voluntarily or forced who could tell, but it could be guessed at. There were definitely different sets, different pay grades or whatever, who worked together. That much she scrambled together.

However, she was haunted by just so much she did not know; all Vix did know for sure was that she had been kidnapped after allowing herself to become so stupidly embroiled in whatever was going on, and her friend had been killed.

She couldn't bear to go on thinking about it, nor could she escape anywhere in her mind for that was where those dreams were, those other lives that plagued her even in this distress, lurking in half sleep. The same recurring faces, the things she seemed to know and understand from that other place and time tormenting her further. She had blamed Dai Stanley, and now here he was.

Vix bit her bottom lip in vexation. She need to be in the here and now.

So, her only hope, her only possible hope, seemed to lie with a man who had used and deceived her and, well now, ditto Dr Stanley. Although it escaped her what the connection could be between the two such opposite individuals, and how exactly he was going to help in any real sense. She almost wanted to laugh. Those two unscrupulous bastards her saviours? Christ!

As she stood there by the window, clutching at her sides, biting her lip and damming herself, she froze. She would recognise those loud clear tones anywhere.

Vix craned her neck trying to look as far as possible out through the drizzled window panes, she had to see.

"Darling," she heard Charlie say.

The guys with the boxes slowed and a few approached her. There was one at her back. Will stepped forward and stared at her. He whispered something to the tallest guy, the one Vix really hated, feared most anyway, and crossed hesitantly towards her. No need. Charlie pulled away from the guard dog with ease and rushed towards him, her arms thrown around his neck, her lips pressed to his, her fingers brushing back his hair.

"Darling," she said once again, her expressive hands playing with Will's hair.

"I wasn't expecting to see you here," his reply was slow, deliberate and chilling.

"I don't know about her," the tall guy said, peering at Will who was releasing himself from Charlie with a very weak smile.

"I'll tell you later," he said with a wink and a bigger beam across his face.

"Now," he demanded, saying something to his compatriot that enlisted his interest and immediate proximity to this new arrival. They eyed her up and down. Charlie showed no sense of intimidation, just those knowing eyes of hers fixing back on them, one to the other and, of course, the smile. Will's shoulders notably relaxed.

Vix looked down at the scene and saw Charlie glance up. They too locked eyes briefly. Will walked away with the men in charge, his arm drooped around them. It didn't look that easy, there was a lot of head-to-head and gesticulating before he smiled conspiratorially with them at last, beckoning Charlie over to join them.

All that Vix could hear was Charlie: light laughter, "Yes, yes, yes, naturally, darling, anything you say, pleasure..."

Vix braced herself as she heard them come inside and she noticed Charlie stare up at the window as she entered before beaming that smile of hers at the men.

As the rain started, Vix sat and contemplated what would, could, happen next.

Although she accepted that Charlie's presence and the kiss she planted on Will was a deliberate act that was undoubtedly meant to help in some way, she still felt disturbed by it. *So, Charlie knew Will all along?* And she certainly heard Dai Stanley talking out on the drive moments before Charlie appeared – so, him too. *All deceit and lies*. They had all played with her thoughts, feelings and ultimately endangered her. She stilled her gratitude at their proximity, they had caused all this; it all trundled through her mind, on that continuous loop that also said they had used her and now that she stood to get in their way they would free her. Or would they? Vix pushed that back, it was the only positive that she could grab onto and she needed it but she ached inside, a cold dull pain throbbing away.

She heard the door open and the stairs start to creak and she drew on that pain, it braced her.

"Upstairs is it? 'Powder my nose' I think the expression is," Charlie laughed loudly as she climbed the stairs, chattering as she went, heels sounding, unhurried.

Vix heard some grunts drifting up through the open door, the treads vibrate and, more than anything, the sound of her own heavy breathing increasing at a rate.

"Be still," she said out loud.

Charlie's heeled footsteps punctuated the silence of the upstairs landing. Vix listened as they went past her door. She heard the bathroom door handle turn, a screech and the drag of the door on the boards. Then she heard singing, Charlie singing at a time like this! Anyone would think she had been drinking, although she had never witnessed that before, far too much control for that; of course they would know that, it was obviously her role. She waited expectantly in what seemed like an age until her own door lock was undone and the handle turned.

Charlie's eyes fixed on Vix.

"Next to the bathroom, go in and go down the backstairs," she mouthed, holding up fingers to her lips to silence any questions Vix might have blurted out.

"Get out and through the back hedge," Charlie continued, smiled very briefly and went leaving the door ajar.

"Sorry, looks like I've interrupted something," she said, fixing the men seated around the table with one of her charming smiles.

Will rose and walked across to her.

"Oh it's OK, darling, I get it, this is work and I'm in the way." She looked up at him and ran her hands down his chest, around his waist, to his pocket. She needed confirmation that he was carrying.

"Well, darling, gentleman," she said, easing away from Will to address the table of drinking men. "I will make a move now."

"Make a move?"

"Yes, toddle off, go, get out of the way, all you men together."

She was calm and the smile never faltered despite their sharp-eyed stares back at her then over to Will, their look interrogatory and piercing.

Charlie casually edged towards the door leading to the hallway, chatting about the time and how she must look and her hair and anything she could generate, just as long as she could get to the door, walking-talking. She clutched her handbag to her and fiddled for a tissue.

"You stay." It was a command.

"Really can't," her smile dropped a little.

"No, just let her go," Will cut across her, walking away as well, open palms out towards them, he leaned slightly forward and mouthed,

"I've had enough of her now."

A couple of the younger lads laughed until cautioned not to by the glances from their two superiors with the palpable hostility they now emitted.

"We do not have a good feeling about this, Jakob, do we Pietre?"

His friend nodded slowly, deliberately, as they both rose steadily, poised.

"What are you saying, guys? You know me! This is a mistake…women."

"Too many mistake, maybe."

"We told we move out. We told be discreet. We told they know about us things…"

“And I know all that too. That’s why she needs to go,” Will seethed through barred teeth before throwing back his head, laughing to the ceiling and rounded on Charlie.

“Get out of here, bitch! See what trouble you’ve caused.”

He spat the words in Charlie’s direction who without hesitation ran.

She hastily pulled the front door closed behind her as she exited. Noticing that the white van on the drive was still occupied, she slowed her pace slightly, just enough, clothing the handle of the revolver in her bag. The engine turned but not before she heard the raised voices from within and as the van pulled away, the sound of gunfire. She ran. It was getting darker, the drizzle hung in the air, water splashed her face as she pressed close by the hedge as it cloaked her back as she followed it round. She needed to get Vix.

Charlie froze as a vehicle passed close by on the road, its dark side practically touching her, but swallowed hard with relief as it wasn’t their van. Charlie stumbled, grabbing the laurel, before steadying herself and retrieving her mobile. She hastily texted Dai Stanley. She hoped he was standing by, she hoped he could be trusted. She could hear movement. She had a final hope that it was Vix.

As Charlie cornered, she could make out the gap that she had pushed her way in to when she had entered the grounds, and she saw Vix through the leaves. She had got out. Made it thus far and Charlie reached for her and pulled at her arm.

“Vix, to me! Quickly, this way.”

Vix pushed herself through then, she saw Charlie, she made out the ditch, she noticed the tarmac of the road and leapt for it regardless of the thrashing branches, the slapping wet leaves and the shouts of the men from the upstairs window.

“Charlie, you saved me,” she gasped as she grabbed her for support.

“Nearly, let’s—”

As Charlie spoke, the men fired from the window, Charlie went for her gun and fired back as she pulled Vix onwards, away from the hedge into the road as a car screeched to a halt beside them.

“Stanley,” Charlie breathed, reaching for the door.

As she pulled Vix in, she heard her sudden scream of pain, more gunfire issuing from above and the sound of feet splashing through the soggy ground.

"Get her in," Dai called from the car, one hand on the wheel, another pointing his revolver out of the car window towards the man visible at the upstairs window.

"Charlie, I," Vix started to speak, then lolled forwards towards Charlie who could only drag her into the back of the revving car, just about closing the door as Dai moved off, got up speed and pushed them back into the seats as he drove.

"Will?" Dai asked, catching Charlie's eye in his mirror. She shook her head.

Dai continued to drive at a pace, getting off the main road as soon as he was able to.

"I might need a hand," Charlie said as she wrestled to get Vix to remain seated upright in the back, trying to keep her awake, to see what injury she had suffered, to see what might be done to help her.

"Vix, now Vix, look at me," Charlie kept speaking to her until there was a response. Vix clasped her arm, shivering and pale, crying noiselessly, in pain, asking why.

"We will take you to a doctor, get you sorted out in no time," Dai Stanley called back to her.

"Yes, that's the plan, hold tight, please try not to worry Vix, try to relax as much as possible."

Vix fixed her with a stare at that, loss of blood and sharp pain had a way of stupefying.

Charlie located the First Aid box and attempted to stem the flow of blood, bandage the wound; just keep her alive was all that she knew she had to do for now. She had no more orders.

"You look very proficient, Charlie. Done this sort of thing much?" Vix voice was weak but clear, and her eyes were sharp. Charlie couldn't quite understand the expression in them, it didn't seem like Vix.

"Have some water," Charlie said, checking Vix's pulse.

"I'm still in a bit of a daze."

"You certainly will be, I'm sure, my dear," Dai said softly, his eyes flickering all about him as they drove, accelerating slowly if a car approached from behind.

"No, I meant about you two. I don't want to sound ungrateful, but, I—" Vix stopped abruptly, wincing as she moved with the car, before leaning forward to project her voice. "I can't get over you two. Finding me, rescuing me. The guns. This, well, get away."

"Vix, please, don't worry yourself now, plenty of time for all that, I'll explain later. Let's get you to that doctor."

"Yes, by all means. But this, this whole thing, you both knowing where I was…" Vix fell silent and rested her head back again before taking a deep breath and waving Charlie away from her. "Let me speak. All this stuff that's been happening. Meeting Will, people, poor Rix being killed. All that regression nonsense playing with my mind."

"Now, calm yourself, dear," Dai cautioned quietly, "some of us have our own beliefs, you know. There is a lot we will discuss."

"No. Do you realise that I actually dream about that other life, back in time… I feel it. I think of those people, of that Will being captured and taken to war. You did that Stanley!" Vix's eyes welled up but she swallowed hard and glared at him through his mirror. She saw him cast down his eyes in avoidance, not shame.

"Vix, we will discuss all this."

"No, Charlie, we will not. I have been completely deceived, by all of you and now I have been shot for Christ's sake. Bloody kidnapped before that! And what is 'Calypso'?"

It was Charlie who looked at Dai through his mirror then.

"You don't understand, Vix."

"Tell me then," Vix glared at Charlie, despite everything she needed to challenge her, what she had done or been party to. Her so called friend.

"There are things, our work, we have to do, for everyone's good. Calypso was a name given to an operation he, I mean Will, was involved in. Sometimes there are, well, let's say casualties…"

Vix briefly smiled to herself, before clutching her arm, her contempt overwhelming. Asking about Calypso made her think of Rix, recall how he had thought he had stumbled on something and she had dismissed him as over dramatic.

"Rix was a 'casualty', was he?" she asked.

Charlie who did not blink.

"Vix, we will talk about all this. We believe."

"What? What do you two believe?"

"Will was working to uncover a gang, drugs, women, you know, modern slavery really, exploitation…"

"Yes, Charlie," she sounded angry at her. "I do know. I'm not that bloody naïve," Vix's voice faltered a little then and she started to cough, holding her arm in agony.

"Well, it was organised crime supporting terrorism, so sometimes there are…"

"People in the way?"

"I don't think you quite grasp matters fully, my dear," Dai interjected, "just leave it to the professionals to make the judgement calls, those that understand the big picture."

Vix despaired of Dai Stanley, his wonderful sense of entitlement, his utter self-belief.

"I'm not discussing anymore with you, either of you," she threw Charlie a warning look. "I'm going to talk to someone I might actually trust, who can really tell me what has been going on, what's been covered up, and who can justify to me why the little guy doesn't matter. You people…"

Vix slumped back, closing her eyes. Dai met Charlie's through the mirror with a nod. She knew what needed to happen and prepared herself.

"Now Vix, please, whatever you say, but let me give you something for the pain."

Vix opened her eyes long enough to see the small loaded syringe going in and Charlie's eyes looking at her intently, only this time filled with tears.

Sometime later…

Gibraltar.

She arrived and took in the heave of the centre, the charm of Rosia Bay with its little houses perched about, some still with old tiled roofs recalling different days. The startling whiteness of the new mosque in the rising mist, seemingly misplaced for any visible community, a more recent intriguing addition to her eye. She traced other pretty shorelines on her progress, old style Italian boats, the storks that claimed their rest, the gangs of apes conspiring together in comradely clumps waiting to pounce.

She wandered alone and unseen, unnoticed by them all as she passed through the old streets and passageways with their little gift shops and cafés. The relentless buzz of motorbikes and revving of cars, the signs for English food and a procession of young Jews behind their leader to an eating house with a large forbidding wooden door despite its displayed menu. The sigh of the tourist busses her only company as she journeyed away from the people, clutching her book from the Gibraltar bookshop.

The same isolation, that certain detachment from the world which worked around her, stalked her as she looked out to sea and as she climbed towards her destination. She walked through the ancient arch, across the undulating roadways and narrow path, found the Trafalgar cemetery; then her mind stepped back in time.

She had found them. Her thoughts were eased, but she didn't know why. There may be resolution in her pilgrimage, but no more answers, for she no longer sought them. They were no longer necessary or needed.

She noticed the repositioned gravestones, read the notices that told some of the story of this place, of the battle, of war and of ignominious disease and death.

Her eyes followed the monuments. She read the inscriptions. She ran her fingers around the contour of a name: Will. Although the reality was that he was a different Will to those she had once, in her other life, encountered.

The gardens were green, water trickled and flowers unfolded in this well-tendered spot. The memory of these long-ago actions and deeds remembered still. Stones shaped the walkways and little benches peppered them, stray cats paraded in the shade of the trees.

She chose her seat and waited. Would he show himself? It had taken a great deal to get this far, so she would stay a while and try to recall him.

A slight breeze caught her cheek and after a moment she turned. Yes, he was coming, he had made it, found her, was actually present, and looking like a relaxed tourist of means with a camera and a baseball style cap, complete with logo.

"Victoria."

She knew that voice but it still shocked her almost to hear it once again. The cadence, the phrasing that gave the last traces of his mother tongue away. It seemed slower and deeper perhaps, but it was him; his tread was light and easy and he clasped his hands together as he neared her, a warm smile growing across his face, his generous mouth curved up, reaching his eyes.

"Shall I sit down?"

She nodded, smiled at his earnestness and thought, despite the physical him, how much like a stranger he seemed at that moment. Would they be able to reclaim it, the trust, she wondered as she beckoned him to be seated next to her, keeping hold of his hand over long, in case; perhaps, she did not want to lose him again.

"You came."

"I said I would. I have always told you that I would return to you. I just needed to find you again. Wait for the right time. You haven't changed, Victoria."

"I had to go, move on, the things that were said about you and then, well."

He removed his cap and inclined his dark head before looking intently at her.

"Do you understand more now? About why I had to leave and why they did and said the things they did?" His eyes burned hers and it saddened her.

"I don't think I will ever fully understand Ashraf, but then I don't feel I fully understand anything anymore, after Operation Calypso snared me in, but you know all about that sort of thing." She released her grasp.

He nodded his agreement: "I've taken early retirement." He smiled, almost bashfully she thought for a moment.

"From being a terrorist or an informer?" She ventured with probing eyes but smiling lips.

"Do you mind which?"

She shook her head and stood up, taking him with her. They walked off together in silence for a while, just the sound of shoes on gravel and the birds above filling in, before she eventually answered.

"I don't know exactly what you might have done, would have done, according to the media etc., not really; and I don't want to know now, because I have heard so much, so many lies, and from people I trusted! But, I do understand what those people are, like those you worked with…" she stopped and put her fingers to his mouth to stop him speaking, "They nearly killed me. I have seen what they can do to people, ordinary people going about their lives, who get in the way," she continued slowly, studying the outline of his shaven face, looking into his dark eyes, searching for the man she had once married.

He might not be there, but then neither was she.

"I had a choice. I nearly took the wrong one. Because of them I didn't, I guess. And, well now, I am content that I have at least found you again, can explain myself to you in person and let you know in here," Ash thumped his chest empathically, "I never left you."

Victoria eyed him and kept walking.

She pictured Charlie. She saw the likes of Will and Dr Stanley. All that sense of entitlement? Certainly clarity of purpose, with right on their side. They knew what they were doing and she, as with anyone else, were expendable. Just as with any zealots.

She remembered Rix, who did not sign up to serve, save others or play the hero. And she thought of that other Will, a young bridegroom with everything to live for, perhaps now at rest beneath her feet. She thought of her own life as well then, ripped apart. Travel through time and nothing changes really, foot soldiers and masters. Trapped by circumstance into taking sides. It was sordid, toxic and dangerous for the little people for sure.

"You said just then that I hadn't changed. Well, actually I really have. I see that I can have a choice, Ash. I want to live, not walk in the shadows anymore. And I choose to believe you. I don't need to know about your motivation. All you have to do is convince me what you can actually offer me now."

Victoria walked, Ash followed and the feral cats circled around the garden's benches.